stories
from under
the sky

stories from under the sky

John Madson

IOWA STATE UNIVERSITY PRESS, *Ames*

I·O·W·A
HERITAGE
COLLECTION

JOHN MADSON, a native of Iowa, now lives in Godfrey, Illinois. He is a full-time writer, specializing in outdoor, natural history, and environmental subjects. He has written many books, most recently *Up on the River*, *Where the Sky Began*, and *Out Home*, and many magazine articles, including articles published in the *Smithsonian*, *Audubon*, and *National Geographic* magazines.

© 1961 Iowa State University Press, Ames, Iowa 50010
All rights reserved

Composed by Iowa State University Press
Printed in the United States of America

No part of this book may be reproduced in any form or by any electronic or mechanical means, including information storage and retrieval systems, without permission from the publisher, except for brief passages quoted in a review.

First edition, 1961
Iowa Heritage Collection edition, 1988

Library of Congress Cataloging-in-Publication Data
Madson, John
    Stories from under the sky / John Madson.
      p. cm.—(Iowa heritage collection)
    ISBN 0-8138-0077-3
      1. Natural history—Middle West. 2. Outdoor life—Middle West. 3. Middle West—Description and travel.   I. Title. II. Series.
QH104.5.M47M33 1988
508.77—dc19
87-34486
CIP

TO HARRY HARRISON
who beckoned from the river

acknowledgment

The author wishes to acknowledge several sources from which many of these stories were drawn. Although a number of the articles in this volume have been altered and rewritten, they exist essentially as they originally appeared in the following publications:

True Magazine: "Half-Ounce Heller." *The Iowa Conservationist*: "The Locks of Medusa," "Outlaw Of The Dark Sloughs," "The Thimble Mill Fox," "Little Brother To The Bear," "The Fighting Doormat," "Geomys," "The Gloomiest Bird," "The Grand Passage," "The Bird Machine," "Child Of Adversity," "Br'er Toad's Secret Weapon," "Waterbugs," "Beware The Paper Cities," "The Unforgettable Feists," and "Sleepers And Snoozers." *The Des Moines Register*: "The World Of Charley Gibbs," "Than A Barrel Of Monkeys," "A Wilderness Of Light," and "Rivers." From *The Mallard,* copyrighted by the Olin Mathieson Chemical Corporation: "Man And The Mallard." *The Drumming Log,* released nationally by the Olin Mathieson Chemical Corporation: "Snake Liars," "The Little Sports," "Knife Talk," "The Small Brown Bird," "Outdoor Wishbooks," "On Crows," and "A Place To Loaf."

PICTURE CREDITS

JACK BRINTON: *Des Moines Register*: pages 148–49

JOHN H. GERARD: page 85

ARNOLD GORE: *Des Moines Register*: page 174

FRANK HEIDELBAUER: page 106

IOWA CONSERVATION COMMISSION: page 23

FRED KENT: pages 116, 117, 118, 121

BOB LONG: *Des Moines Register*: pages 89, 92

LEONARD LEE RUE III: pages 26, 32

C. W. SCHWARTZ: pages 19, 24, 25, 36, 39, 42, 52, 54, 57, 59, 63, 134, 138, 153, 160, 191

JIM SHERMAN: page 51

The drawings which appear throughout the book and on the jacket were all prepared by DYCIE MADSON.

contents

MAMMALIA

The Thimble Mill Fox	11
Little Brother to the Bear	17
A Songdog at Work	23
Half-ounce Heller	27
Sleepers and Snoozers	37
The Fighting Doormat	43
Than a Barrel of Monkeys	49
Geomys	55
Fawns	61

THE RIVER

Old Man River's Shell Game	67
Outlaw of the Dark Sloughs	81
The World of Charlie Gibbs	87

AVES

The Gloomiest Bird	99
The Grand Passage	103
Man and the Mallard	107

The Bird Machine 115
Child of Adversity 123
Heron Summer 127

THE UNLOVED

Br'er Toad's Secret Weapon 135
Waterbugs 139
The Turtle Hunters 143
Beware the Paper Cities! 151
The Locks of Medusa 157

SHORT ARROWS FROM THE LONG BOW

The Abashed Savage 167
Snake Liars 169
The Little Sports 171
A Wilderness of Light 175
Rivers 179
The Unforgettable Feists 181
Knife Talk 185
Froze Fer Meat 187
On Crows 189
Romany Rides Again 193
The Small Brown Bird 199
Outdoor Wishbooks 201
A Place To Loaf 203

mammalia

the thimble mill fox

FROM FAR DOWN the valley came the first trail cry of the pack.

For a long time there had been only muted hunting noises from the Walkers as they cast through the creek valleys for fox scent. But as they swung between a bottomland corn patch and Thimble Mill, the gaunt hound leading the pack gave voice — a ringing bawl that floated across the dark valleys and ridges of the night, up to the cold stars and beyond, and back to the hilltop where three men sat by a fire.

"Listen!" said one. He stood stiffly, a long spare figure in a sheepskin coat. "They done raised him!"

Another hound-bawl, dim with distance, joined the first. Then, from the black ridges that stretched below the listening men, there rang a dissonant chorus ending with the cat-like squalls of foxhounds striking trail.

The men listened and drank their coffee while the sounds steadied to the level, consistent trail cry. A thin, frosty moon hung above them and a November wind blew through the naked oaks around them.

"That was my Drive dog," said the tall man, drawing his coat closer. "Git your money ready — my dog give first tongue!"

"If that's your Drive dog give first tongue," said the man from Protem, "this night's gonna be hell on possums. You just know that's Ed's Mose dog."

"Ain't neither one," the third man said. "I do believe it's one of Nancy's pups. I don't think Drive has left the crick yet. He's likely got a crawdad treed down there."

"Oh, you're powerful talkers," said the tall man sourly. "Stop jawin' and listen!"

On cue, the baying of the hunting hounds broke around the spur of a distant hill.

A mile away they ran in a loose line, their tails held like scimitars and their nostrils flared with the rank scent that hung just above the earth. It was a wet autumn and fox spoor held well to sodden leaves and grass, a band of smell that led the hounds down to the valley floor, through the branch, through the horseweeds and catbriar beyond it, and along the oak-grown shoulders of Jericho Township.

The young dog was leading, and with every stride he gave tongue. Behind him ran his dam, the splendid little Walker bitch named Squealer, and in her steps came the other four hounds. They spurned spring branch and hollow, flashed by patches of brush and pasture, through black peninsulas of timber and out into the dim light of frosty cornfields.

"I make that dog now," said the tall man studiedly. "It's young Sidemeat And Runnin' Gears. Hear that little break?"

The third man, head canted and mouth opened slightly to absorb the far baying, said: "They cuttin' back already?"

"Still headin' for the river, sounds like."

"No, they ain't. There! Hear that?"

Under a distant ridge, at the foot of a cedar-split ledge that no human had seen for forty years — a place that caught the night and thickened it, vesting it with the smells of wet stone, copperheads, and maidenhair fern — the trail cry of the dogs lost its rhythm. Little Squealer, as she cast up the creek bank, squalled in frustration. She was joined by Blue and Clabberbutt, and then by Sidemeat And Runnin' Gears. It was the grizzled Drive on the far bend of the creek — the old sire with the slit ears and the broken tail — that gave the rallying call to his pack. The dogs fought through freezing mud to join him, and by the time they had crossed the creek Drive had taken up the trail cry again.

A half-mile ahead, laughing to himself and with his red-orange brush flying, ran the fox. Like Drive, he was an old dog and the veteran of a hundred hunts. He knew his work well, knowing the ways of hounds and how to tangle a trail for young, foolish dogs. He could run all night and all day and when he tired there was always the home den above Thimble Mill. Until then he would deceive and bedevil the dogs. There were creeks to kill his trail scent and barnyards to mask it, and if he chose he might even show the hounds some fancy rail-walking on an old fence or two.

Full-coated and in splendid condition, he had not eaten since the night before. With belly empty and feet light, he could run forever — run grinning beyond any hound or man, running without weight or weariness down the watersheds and ridges that he had ranged a thousand times. This was home country and he would tangle it for the dogs, weaving a web of confusion and outrage for the dogs, running weightlessly through the leagues of mountain night with tongue lolling and black-hosed legs spurning every hogback, hollow and spring branch in the Township of Jericho.

"Didn't your wife name that pup 'Lucky'? How come you call him 'Sidemeat And Runnin' Gears'?"

"You got eyes. That's about all he is — ribs, chest and laigs."

"And nose and mouth," added the tall man. "He's a likely dog, that one."

For two hours the Walkers had coursed the fox. The scent still hung hot and heavy before them but their first trail cries had settled down to a serious, business-like tonguing. Like the fox they could run forever, baying through Jericho until the pads were torn from their feet or the fox was put to earth. It was a night for running and their breaths streamed behind them, the hunting fever burning.

Through the timber, along the ridges, in icy mud and past clay bluffs by the creeks, by the elms and under the oaks, with whole sections of land and mountainsides fading behind in the frosty moonlight, ran the hounds. With legs of steel and chests like kegs, they held the rank fox smell in their nostrils and drove down it like a highroad. A swollen-necked buck crashed away up a slope, leaving the musky stench of the Rutting Moon in the laurel thickets. A pair of raccoons, crayfishing in the stone shingle of Pester Fork, shambled high-rumped to their den tree, *chirr-r-ring* angrily and leaving their scent on the gravel.

The hounds struck these spoors, and also the dust bath of a turkey flock and the scent post of an emigrant coyote. A mile below the Fork they cut the trail of a bobcat — the sweetish reek of a huge tom that had bounded noiselessly up the high ledges and vanished into blank rock. These smells were summarily noted, analyzed and discarded by Drive and Squealer. For a moment, when they had struck the heady musk of the big buck, the younger hounds had faltered and nearly turned. But the old dogs, unswerving, drew them along with leashes of blood and discipline, running strong down the trail of the Thimble Mill Fox.

There was suddenly a mass of big dark shapes before them that rose up sleepily, lowing in alarm. The young hounds blundered in among the cows, confused and milling, but Sidemeat and Drive sensed the trick and swung around the herd to pick up the trail beyond.

Three hours. The men on the ridge had not heard their dogs for a long time and were drinking scalding coffee and storying to each other as dog men will.

"So I told him not to fret," the man from Protem was saying. "His dog would turn up. Always had. Been lost a dozen times and always turned up. But Dan, he says: 'No, that good dog of mine is gone this time. I just feel it!'

"Aw, Dan, I says, he's just sommers out in the hills, chasing a bitch. 'No he ain't,' says Dan, 'because he's a bitch hisself!'"

"That's Dan Buckles, right enough," grinned the tall man. "You mind the time he went to a sale and swapped a brood sow for that big Trigg dog he's got? His wife carried on just terrible. Says: 'Dan, have you taken leave of your wits? Trading a fine brood sow for a dog?' Dan looks at her with that way of his and says: 'Old woman, I've lived with you for thutty years and I always figured you had good sense. But you know dam good and well that I cain't run no fox with a three-hunnert-pound sow!'"

The Protem man flung back his head and brayed with laughter, and was just remembering another story when the faint, full-throated cry of the pack burst in on him.

"They've swung him around. Comin' in below us!"

"There's Drive again. There's that Joker pup, and old Squealer. Where's Sidemeat?"

"If he's gone crooked again, I'll shoot that Sidemeat dog!"

"No — hark to him! Say boys, don't you know that ol' fox is gettin' a bellyful tonight!"

The red flag of the fox was still high and defiant but somewhere — maybe the last time he had circled the Township — the fun had gone out of it. He had a year's running left in him in weather like this but the slender, spring steel legs — undisciplined by man or bloodline — were losing temper and the mountain miles began to sap will and purpose. His belly fur was clotted with mud and burrs, an intolerable thing that no fox can be expected to endure. There must be grooming tonight and hunting tomorrow, and so home to the ridge above Thimble Mill.

The men stood now, spellbound by the patient chopping of their iron dogs. Hour after hour, drumming along the frozen ridges and breasting the tangles of laurel and serviceberry, the dogs drove down the trail of the fox. The noise faded up a dark valley, and again rang faint and bell-like through the gathering frost. There was a single bawl far up the valley to the north and a brief clamor that the men strained to hear.

"He's gone to ground, and about time," said the tall man, pouring himself one last cup of black coffee.

"I'll call them in," said the man from Protem, lifting his steerhorn trumpet. Over the valleys and whitening meadows floated the mellow, booming come-home call of the old foxhunter.

The dogs, milling happily around the den above the creek, lifted their heads. The pups drew away first, followed by old Drive and Squealer, and for the first time that night they left the rank vulpine scent and turned back to the firelit hilltop and home.

After a while the fox slept. The moon was down, and where the black valleys and hogbacks had rung with dog music there were now only the sounds of the wind high in the oaks. The men, the dogs and the fire were gone, and so was the coffee.

little brother to the bear

SHAMBLING THROUGH our dense river forests in the easy, flat-footed fashion of the bear, goes an American legend.

He was the reluctant haberdasher for a pioneer era, furnishing warm headgear to several generations of frontiersmen, and coloring our folklore with Old Zip 'Coon, the Bearcat, Br'er 'Coon, and the Ringtailed Whizzard. He's the raccoon, the black-masked, high-rumped, hound-scarring little hero of the autumn valleys.

His specific name, *lotor,* is Latin for "the washer." Around water, especially in captivity, he may dip bread or other soft food until it almost disappears. Several 'coons dipping food in a small pan of water can reduce it to a semi-liquid gruel, losing most of the original meal in the process. Even a frog or crayfish — freshly taken from clean water — may be repeatedly dunked.

No one has ever doped this out. Away from water, the 'coon takes his food as he finds it, sans dipping. Some naturalists think it's just because the raccoon likes to mess around water, and others suspect that the raccoon likes to feel submerged food with its sensitive hands. One authority says simply: "Perhaps this sensitivity is an obsession, just as some beavers seemingly hope to flood the world."

But this is the sort of thing you'd expect from the raccoon. He's a character that stands apart in a forest of characters and even more than most wild animals, he has a burning itch to investigate the universe.

I once went into a cageful of eighty young raccoons to stir them up for a photographer. As soon as I stepped into the big cage, the curious little ringtails swarmed all over me. They pulled my hair, untied my shoes, stole my pencil, pulled out the foil on a pack of cigarettes, and almost got away with my lighter. They were in pockets, after buttons, and generally making pests of themselves.

It wasn't until early that evening that I noticed the 'coons had even found the shiny metal tab of my trousers zipper. I'd been running errands in downtown stores half the afternoon with my britches agap.

This sharp fascination with shiny objects often leads to raccoon disaster. A time-honored trapping method is to cover a trap's pan with shiny tinfoil and place the trap in clear, shallow water at the edge of gravel or rock riverbars where raccoons hunt crayfish. 'Coons can't resist anything strange or shiny; like kids, they usually get into trouble by picking up things. Their long, black dextrous "fingers" are capable of grasping objects and manipulating them. While the 'coon does not have the opposable thumb of man and the higher primates, he does right well. For most practical purposes, he has hands.

With these sensitive "hands" he can grope under rocks and along margins of streams for crayfish and frogs. He may eat snails and mussels, or tear apart rotten logs for worms and grubs. Raccoons will eat birds' eggs, and there is one record

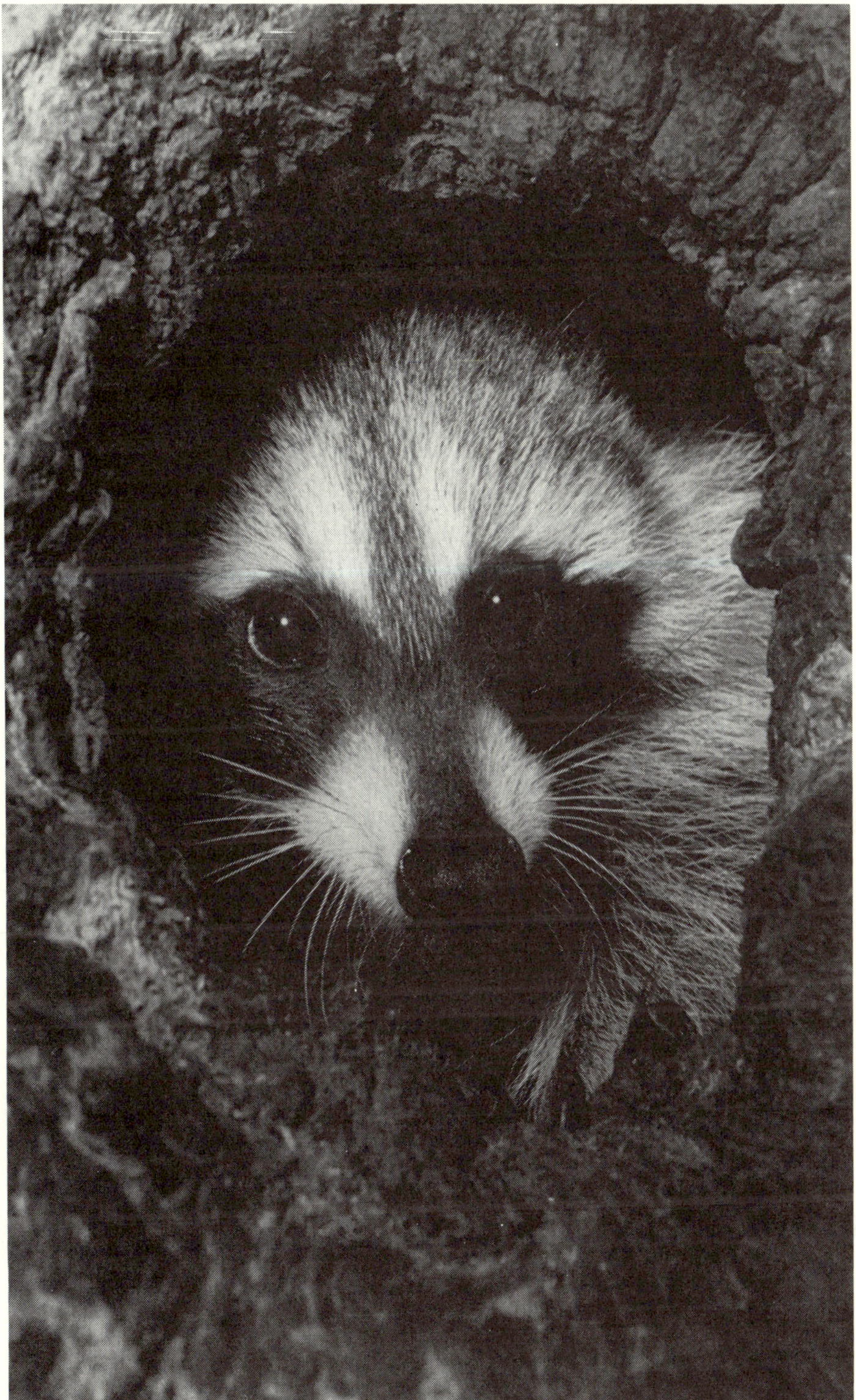

of a 'coon climbing sixty feet to a redtailed hawk's nest, eating the eggs, and then curling up in the nest and falling asleep. There may have been some big doings when Ma Hawk came home.

Although raccoons are more closely related to the pandas, they are often compared to the bears. Like bears, raccoons are omnivorous and will eat anything from honey to sweet corn to ants. Like bears, they are plantigrade — walking flat-footed. And, like some bears, they may choose to die facing the enemy.

A big male raccoon can be very rough if he's pushed beyond his patience, and a large female 'coon with young can be a terror. There's an old hunting yarn that raccoons lead pursuing hounds into deep water and kill them by climbing on their heads and drowning them. If this is fiction, it's at least universal, for it is believed by many old hunters. It is certainly possible. A raccoon is an excellent swimmer, very strong, and is well-armed. They're big enough to give a dog a very rough time. Large boar 'coons here in the corn country are commonly said to weigh 35 pounds and more, and you'll hear unverified reports of northern raccoons that go nearly 50 pounds. But that's coming it awful strong. It's like the stories of 100-pound beavers and 25-pound Canada ganders — everyone has heard of such giants and believes in them, but no one ever seems to really see them. I've seen a "35-pound" raccoon placed on parcel post scales; it was a great old boar 'coon that weighed a few ounces over 28 pounds. But everything's relative. If you follow the hounds for a few hours, and then carry a 25-pound raccoon five or six miles through midnight forest, you may think he weighs 60 pounds by the time you see hot coffee again.

Most raccoons, however, probably weigh from 10 to 20 pounds and are at their heaviest when they go into winter. Although raccoons put on a lot of tallow for winter, they do not hibernate in the true sense but may sleep for days at a time when winter really cracks down and life is at its grimmest. Unlike hibernating groundhogs, wintering raccoons — like bears — have no sharp drop of body temperature or pulse rate and if disturbed during their winter naps they can awaken instantly.

A lot of this winter sleeping is done in hollow den trees and hollow logs. In summer, raccoons seem to like taking their daytime naps in the open, preferably in the sun if it isn't hot weather. Most 'coons nap by day and hunt by night, and the midday siestas are usually taken on high. It's not uncommon for raccoons to sleep in lofty crows' nests, although they're usually found on broad, high limbs or in large tree forks. A squirrel season never passes when I don't see at least one 'coon in the top of a high snag or a heavy limb, peering sleepily down as I walk by. Many of these appear to be young animals, and they show more curiosity than fear.

Agile and sure-footed, raccoons are as much at home in trees as any squirrel. If they decide to leave a tree they can leap from alarming heights without apparent injury. Twice I have seen desperate raccoons weighing at least 20 pounds do this. In one instance the 'coon jumped from a limb over thirty feet above the ground without even having the breath knocked from him, leaping beyond the dogs and climbing a large den tree nearby before they could take him. In the other case, a very large raccoon made a twenty-foot high dive into a river and escaped.

There has been a peculiar recession and advance of the raccoon front. A hundred years ago they were common in much of the northern midwest and northeast, especially around watercourses, and were a staple food of the Indians. With civilization, they vanished from many parts of their original range, as did the deer, turkey and beaver. But — just as the deer, turkey and beaver — they've made a strong comeback. In 1900, for example, raccoons were rare in Iowa, eastern Nebraska and South Dakota, and southern

Minnesota. But the raccoons started to reappear in the 1920's and early 1930's. They began to occur in trappers' catches again, although to most trappers a raccoon remained far more unusual than a mink. But since the late 1920's raccoons have steadily built up in the northern midwest, just as they have in parts of Maine and New England, and they are now a very common game species in nearly all parts of the nation.

The present status of the raccoon has been attained in only the past thirty years in the north, and what depressed the 'coon population before that is not known. Maybe the comeback was made under protection, or because the raccoon had ceased being an important game animal and part of local hunting tradition. Perhaps there were subtle but important changes in the environment that made the resurgence possible. Whatever the reason, Br'er 'Coon is back and thousands of northern hunters are glad of it.

Raccoons are invariably hunted with trailing hounds, the object being to tree the 'coon before he can reach the asylum of a den. This may take some doing because old 'coons are masters at tangling trails, playing the water game in creeks, and taking to tree travel.

The damp, chilly nights of November are best for this sort of thing, the apple cider nights of late fall when raccoon scent hangs strong and pungent and the woods are hushed and waiting for winter.

There are coal oil lanterns swinging under the hill, and men cussing the catbriars and grapevines that trip them up and detain them from the chase. Up the river bottom and far ahead, there are hounds singing down a crooked trail.

And leading this November parade, growling and *chirring* under his breath and getting fit to comb some burrs out of a few upstart hounds — as American as bayberry candles and puncheon floors — is Old Zip 'Coon himself.

On a summer prairie — in the manner sometimes employed by wolves that hunt by day — a mother coyote waits patiently in the thin shade of a thorntree. Far away, beside a small clump of yellow brome sedge, something moves. The coyote is instantly alert, her keen eyes, ears and nostrils straining to define the movement and weigh the possibility of a kill.

a songdog

There is a careful stalk, a scrambling rush, and a cottontail rabbit is started. The rabbit is a famous runner, artful, nimble and capable of covering twenty feet in a single second, but on open ground he cannot match the endurance and speed of the coyote.

The rabbit is overrun, tumbled along the grass, and caught and killed before it can regain its feet.

at work

An ancient melodrama has been played out, with an ending as old as the prairie itself. A rabbit dies, and a new generation of coyote pups is being weaned in the den behind the ridge.

Incessantly hungry, and fearing nothing that crawls, the shrew will not hesitate to attack small snakes. This small garter snake was no match for the shrew, and was swiftly killed and eaten.

half-ounce heller

IN SOME OF the quiet places, where leaf mold is heavy and old logs decay on the forest floor, lives the world's most savage mammal. It's a ravening little beast seldom seen by man; an irascible, twittering phantom that kills incessantly. Even the weasels and great cats can't match its talent for bloodletting, for each day it must devour its own weight in food, or starve.

But the same nature that grants a genius for death always stops short of fatal perfection. This terrible hunter — the shrew — may weigh no more than a dime.

What the shrew lacks in brawn, however, it makes up in sheer brass. Not that it is brave; fear and bravery are relative qualities that the shrew can't afford. It just doesn't have time. Every waking hour is spent in either mating or hunting, and any fear or discretion that might dwell in the tiny brain is pretty well eclipsed by an eternal, lion-sized appetite.

It's a far-flung breed, but you can spend years in the woods and grasslands without seeing a shrew. Sometime you may hear a birdlike twitter in the grass or a transient scuttling in the leaves that you just write off as some sort of bug. That's a shrew for you — all business, no show.

One fall day a big fox squirrel and I were sweating each other out and I'd been watching the distant elm for maybe twenty minutes, quietly cussing the deer flies in my hair, when I caught a flash of something under the gooseberry bush beside me. There was a small dun shape that flickered across the patch of bare dirt under the bush and vanished into a drift of fallen leaves beyond. A few seconds later it reappeared, a tiny spark of an animal that paused there, nose high, for one frozen instant.

It looked like a miniature mouse that had been whittled to a point. There was a long, sharp muzzle and I can't recall seeing any eyes or ears. The entire animal wouldn't have gone more than four inches, including the mouselike tail. But what struck me most about the little critter was the almost electric quality of tension; the shrew seemed to carry its own field of vibrating energy and although it obviously knew there was a huge animal nearby, I'd swear that its only interest in me was as a food item, not an enemy. It tasted the air, decided I wasn't for the eating, and buzzed off into the leaves again.

At such a snap glance — which is usually all you get — a shrew's resemblance to a mouse is marked. But there is no kinship; a shrew is an insectivore, not a rodent, and has a mouthful of canines to prove it. Mice are bigger and bulkier, with longer legs, coarser fur and larger ears. A shrew might also be taken for a young mole in high gear, but it's much more active than any mole and its forelegs aren't greatly developed by digging.

They say that when a shrew isn't hungry he's fairly easy to get along with. I wouldn't know. I've never seen one that wasn't hungry. They're usually tormented little beasts, all teeth and belly.

Dr. C. Hart Merriam, the great zoologist, once confined a hungry shrew with a large whitefooted mouse. The shrew weighed eleven grams, the mouse went seventeen.

The shrew quickly became aware of something else in the cage and gave chase. The mouse's great agility made escape easy and he often hurdled the shrew as he scampered frantically about the cage. The shrew's bad eyesight gave it trouble, and the little killer once passed two inches from the mouse without seeing it.

But the shrew kept doggedly at it and flushed the mouse again and again, slowly wearing it down. The mouse "showed evidence of extreme terror."

After several minutes of this the shrew finally caught the mouse's tail and was jerked and dragged violently around the cage until he was torn loose. A little later he connected again and seized the mouse by the side and the two rolled over, fighting fiercely. Again the mouse freed itself, but was so exhausted that the shrew easily caught it and locked its tiny teeth in an ear. In spite of the rodent's maddened kicks and bites, the shrew happily began eating the ear of its victim. Once more the mouse broke free but the shrew quickly caught it and resumed work on the ear.

When the ear was gone the shrew clambered up on the mouse's back, cut through the skull, and began on the brain. He ate this, the whole side of the head and part of the shoulder at one sitting. The shrew had been half an hour in wearing its victim down, and another half hour in killing it. During this time he never gave up, but kept at the job with grim dedication.

This lethal persistence is carried on with no apparent fuss or bravado on the shrew's part. There's little noise. It's just a matter of getting supper underway as quickly as possible and it's immaterial to the shrew whether his victim is dead or alive when he does it.

As if ferocity wasn't enough, the shrew has another

weapon that shades the battle equipment of all other higher mammals. It is one of the few warm-blooded creatures on earth that has a poisonous bite.

All mammals may inflict tooth or claw wounds that induce sepsis, and the bite of no wild creature should be ignored by a human victim. But that's a matter of infection. Some shrews actually have venom glands.

Their poison stems from an unusual group of salivary cells in the lower jaw and is most powerful in the genus *Blarina,* the short-tailed shrews. This poison is thought to be powerful enough to kill a human being if injected in quantity directly into the bloodstream. Happily, efficient injection equipment is lacking in the shrews. The tiny, needle-like teeth of the shrew just aren't capable of putting the poisonous saliva where it counts, except in insects and other small prey. The mechanism is apparently adequate to knock off a mouse but not a rabbit.

This poisonous trait of the shrew is one of those things that has been accepted and debunked off and on through the years. Centuries ago, Europeans believed that the shrews packed a toxic wallop, and old-time Britons even thought a shrew running over a foot could cause serious lameness and pain.

In Edward Topsell's *Historie of Foure Footed Beasts,* published in old London, the writer noted: "It (the shrew) is a ravening beaste feygning itselfe to be gentle and tame, but being touched it biteth deepe, and poisoneth deadly." That was in 1607; in later years the proposition of a venomous mammal couldn't quite be bought by an expanding zoology and the age of reason.

In my old *Buffon's Natural History,* circa 1810, that great naturalist wrote: "The aversion of the house cat to the shrew mouse gave rise to the notion that this is a venomous animal and that its bite is dangerous. The truth, however, is that it is neither venomous nor capable of biting...."

A shrewd observer, Buffon was a little too previous in

kicking the venom theory. And it's a cinch that he never handled shrews with his bare hands. On the strength of his last point I once picked up a masked shrew with my naked fingers. I still respect Buffon, but I have news for him.

Even early in this century, some scholars were hesitant to attribute venomous qualities to the shrews. A well-known eastern naturalist helped dispel their doubts in the most direct way. While capturing a short-tailed shrew, C. J. Maynard was bitten on the hand. Within thirty seconds he felt a severe burning sensation and shooting pains that extended up the arm. The pain and swelling reached their climax in about an hour, but Maynard could not use the affected hand without great suffering for three days, and felt considerable discomfort for more than a week.

If little *Blarina* had the hypodermic dentition of the pit vipers, it might give man a very bad time. Extracts from the poison cells have been injected into mice and proved highly lethal. Extremely small quantities of this extract have killed three-pound rabbits within five minutes. It requires only six milligrams of the stuff to kill small mice and it's been found that the salivary glands of a single shrew contain enough venom to kill 200 mice. The poison is most virulent in the short-tailed species, and is less potent in others. Saliva of the long-tailed shrews, for example, appears to have only a slight crippling effect on their victims.

Equipped with a mouthful of reddish-brown teeth and a supply of venomous saliva, the short-tailed shrew is a masterful little butcher, even of its own kind. That's the way it must be. As the world's smallest mammals, shrews have the highest metabolism and energy consumption. They simply blaze through life; the masked shrew, for example, is reported to breathe 850 times a minute and has a pulse rate of 800.

This takes a lot of fuel. Dr. Merriam once placed three shrews under a water tumbler. The little warriors had at it immediately. In a few minutes one had been killed and

A brace of deadly items — a short-tailed shrew and a shotgun shell that is only 2¾ inches high.

eaten by the others, and one of these was later killed and eaten by his companion. When it was all over, Dr. Merriam gravely commented that the survivor "was greatly distended."

The shrews' diet is anything small enough to be killed — grubs, worms, small salamanders, mice and other creatures found in leaf litter, surface soil, logs or old stumps. Shrews will eat carrion, too, and if it's alive with maggots they will eat the maggots. Not rangy enough to take an alert mouse in the open, the shrew can corner mice in burrows and kill them easily. The thick skins of many shrews, particularly in the neck region, are virtually mouseproof.

Until recently, some of the tinier species have been almost unknown in some parts of their ranges because of the difficulty in collecting and describing them. Most shrews are difficult to take alive. If the trap is in the sun, they may die quickly of sunstroke. If the weather is wet or chilly, they may die of exposure. If you don't get there soon enough, they may just die of starvation.

Most of the shrews I've seen in the field have been dead ones. I've found several in the woods, especially while hunting arrowheads or fish bait or anything else that kept me close to earth. Some of the dead shrews were apparently unmarked, as if they had simply keeled over in mid-scuttle. Maybe they had just worn themselves out. It can happen. Driven mercilessly by that fiery metabolism, a shrew eats too often and lives too fast. It drives itself at an impossible pace, and shrews may be found without mark of injury or violence, dead of old age at sixteen months.

Recent studies of some of these "burnt-out" shrews reveal that they may have been done in by other creatures, and they may actually show signs of rough handling beneath their untorn skins. Hawks and owls hunt shrews regularly and eat them. Cats and other mammals, however, don't seem too interested in eating shrews after they kill them. Why?

The answer lies in a substance that is extremely offensive to many predatory animals. Hawks, owls and other raptors, not having a sense of smell, don't mind. But mammals do. The short-tailed shrew — the one with the serious saliva — gives off a particularly powerful odor from oily skin glands situated on each side and along the midline of the belly. He's got everything, that boy. The odor emitted from these glands becomes stronger when the shrew is injured, excited or angry, and while a dog or cat may casually slay a shrew, they must be more than casually hungry to eat it.

None of our shrews are large, but they have a sweeping range and are found almost anywhere in North America in moist, temperate situations. Some, however, occur in the far north and in the drier parts of sagebrush country.

The short-tailed shrew is found everywhere in the eastern United States from the central Dakotas and east Texas to the Atlantic. It's big as shrews go, with head and body measuring up to four inches.

Water shrews are also large, with head and body lengths of about three and one-half inches. This shrew occurs in only a few of the northern and western states and is reported to be the only mammal that can walk on water. According to some naturalists, it may hold air bubbles on its feet and run quickly and easily for short distances across the surfaces of quiet pools. It can swim, dive and walk on stream bottoms in its quest for food. Underwater, the thick, plushy fur traps air bubbles and the shrew appears to be sheathed in silver.

Bob Olive and I were fishing for steelheads in the Baptism River up Duluth way one spring when a tiny animal flashed into a small pool nearby and swam quickly across to an alder bog beyond. Not a very smart move in steelhead water, but he made it. The fact that any shrew can swim underwater is astounding, considering the metabolism and attendant high respiratory rate. A shrew swimming underwater is roughly comparable to a sprinter running a two-minute mile and then skin-diving for abalones to cool off.

A few north-central states have the pygmy shrew, the New World's smallest mammal. They're seldom seen; they're fairly rare everywhere and aren't hard to overlook, for an adult pygmy shrew weighs about as much as a new dime, with a head and body only two inches long. It can travel in the tunnels of large beetles and the burrows dug by this tiny animal may be too small to admit a common pencil! Until a short time ago this was believed to be the world's smallest mammal, but a species recently found in Africa has the new title.

For all these spectacular traits, the shrews are virtually unknown to most outdoorsmen. We ignore the more unapparent reptiles, mammals and birds and our fancies are best caught and held by creatures that we can kill or eat, or that can kill and eat us. In our airy world of sky and sun we overlook the ecological niches of things like shrews and regard ourselves as the most fearsome of creatures.

All this ends at our shoe soles. In the world between the soil and the sun, the shrew is king. He is the terror of terrors within his range, a destroyer that is never slaked nor fed. Knowing no peace himself during his brief life, he grants it to nothing else in that violent, half-lit land of the grassroots and leaf mold.

Talk about your fighting bulls, rogue tuskers and other brutes that run to high tonnage. But thank the red gods that the common shrew doesn't weigh a hundred pounds!

A jumping mouse, yanked out of his dried-grass bed by a prying biologist, is still sound asleep, curled in a tight ball and oblivious to the world until spring. Nose is tucked between hind legs, and the long tail neatly encircles the head.

sleepers and snoozers

THE OLD WOODCHUCK labored slowly up the hill, breathing heavily and stopping often to rest. He was hog-fat now that late September had come, and with each passing day he grew lazier and more somnolent.

Although the sun still swung high in the south and the noontimes were warm, something in his dim mind spoke of winter. So, rolling ponderously, he entered his hillside tunnel late one afternoon and left Indian summer behind.

In a daze the 'chuck moved to the end of a long passage to a chamber almost filled with dried grass. With the last of his wakefulness he scraped dirt from the chamber wall and packed it at the entrance, sealing himself from the main tunnel and entombing himself for the winter. His energy spent, he rolled into a ball and slept.

More than sleep, it was almost death, a coma that would be broken only by the south winds of early March that warmed the soil of the hillside. The old groundhog was so tightly curled that his lungs were compressed and breathing became only a faint trickle of air through his nostrils. His pulsebeat faded and slowed, his body temperature dropped forty-five degrees, and winter beat unheard at the mouth of the tunnel.

Above the 'chuck's den at the pasture edge, a thirteen-striped ground squirrel had retired a month earlier. During the summer the little federation squirrel — named for his thirteen stripes — had become so fat that his belly almost touched the ground. Although he'd frolicked in the broiling sun of July and August, the heat of mid-September had grown strangely oppressive and one day the ground squirrel retreated to the coolness of his burrow, not to reappear until the following April.

Nearly three-fourths of the ground squirrel's life was to be spent in deep sleep. In the deathlike torpor his pulse slowed from 200 beats a minute to only 5. He was safe from winter in his nest of grass, for the temperature of the home burrow was far above that of the outside world. But, just in case, the squirrel was equipped with a metabolic thermostat and if the den temperature dropped a deadly four or five degrees below freezing the sleeper would awaken and his body temperature would rise almost at once. But for this, he would die.

Across the river in a limestone crevice, hanging up in bed, was a brown bat. During the summer days he had slept in safety and darkness in the same fissure, battening on flying insects at night. As the days shortened and the temperature in the crevice dropped to forty degrees, the bat became drowsy and joined his neighbors in sleep.

Except for a rare movement and a breath every five minutes, the little flier might have been dead. His heartbeat nearly ceased, and his blood supply fell as his spleen grew large and congested with red blood corpuscles. Once or twice during the winter, perhaps, something might stimulate the bat into wakefulness and a reflex action of the swollen spleen would pour red blood cells back into circulation, increasing the oxygen charge in his blood and permitting increased activity. He might even lap condensation from the stone wall beside him. If the crevice became too cold and untenable, he might fly considerable distances in search of warmer quarters. If such quarters are not found, and soon, the bat must die of exposure and starvation.

Below on the valley floor, the jumping mouse had called it a year and retired. In late summer he had grown so fat that he could hardly hop about on his kangaroo legs, and he finally gave up sleepily and burrowed into a mound of soft soil. Sealing his tunnel behind him, he carefully arranged a coverlet of leaves and grass about himself and balled up with his head tucked between his hind legs, his long tail curled neatly around him. He is now cold as death to the touch, insensible to pain, and if one of his small

A jumping mouse, fattened for winter and ready for hibernation.

toes is excised the wound does not bleed. He will not appear above-ground again for seven months.

These are some of the true sleepers, the mammals that seldom know winter.

There are other mammals that join them briefly, sleeping through the worst of it, but which never attain the near-death of the true hibernators. These might be called the snoozers.

The opossum is typical, dozing through much of the winter but occasionally wandering out of his warm burrow or hollow tree in the coldest weather. It's hard for 'possums to understand anything — even winter — and they may literally freeze their tails off. An opossum's naked tail has little protection against a January cold snap, and I have treed spring 'possums that had only blackened stumps in place of their handy, prehensile tails.

The 'possum's sleeping quarters may be almost anywhere, and are never invested with much effort. Winter or summer, Br'er Possum is a dull creature; he may winter in hollow trees or an old squirrel's nest or share a burrow with another animal that's indifferent to his carrion smell — usually a skunk. The 'possum brings his own bedding, curling his tail on the ground, filling the loop with dead leaves, and dragging this into the burrow. Although he sometimes gets out of bed during winter, he often remains inactive and torpid for weeks during very cold weather.

A similar pattern is followed by the skunk, raccoon and badger — spending the summer growing fat and much of the winter lazing in some snug den. These mammals do not hibernate, and will eat if something turns up. In late winter, male skunks can be kept at home only by sub-zero temperatures. Although the heavily-larded badger will seal off his bedroom from the drafty entrance tunnel, he may make short hunting trips into the white world of the prairie winter.

The man on the street, if he bothers to think about it, may regard hibernation as an acquired defense against winter cold. But if this is so, why do woodchucks hibernate before the first hard frost, and why do some ground squirrels begin their long sleep in late summer?

Is it a defense against starvation during the leanest months of the year? This might be true in the case of the insectivorous bats that have but two choices in late autumn: migrate or hibernate. But how can one explain those rodents that enter hibernation when food is plentiful and easily available? And why does the thirteen-striped ground squirrel — one of the most profound sleepers — persist in storing food for the winter?

There is a theory that hibernation is triggered by an autonarcosis, and that hibernants drug themselves with an excess of carbon dioxide in the blood. A typical hibernation torpor has been induced in woodchucks by forcing them to breathe air high in carbon dioxide content. Confined air has also hastened hibernation when ground squirrels were placed in cans that were tightly sealed except for a few small nail holes. These animals hibernate much sooner than those in highly-perforated cans of the same size. But why would the burrows of some animals be relatively more confining than others, or why would those animals — the hibernators — be more sensitive to confinement?

To any rule that might be drawn concerning hibernation, there is an exception to confound the issue. The phenomenon is not restricted to such herbivores as the rodents, for many of the insectivorous bats are hibernators. And even among the true sleepers, there are such exceptions as the eastern chipmunks. One chipmunk may sink into the typically deep torpor of the true hibernant; another individual may remain active in deep January.

Hibernation is one of those natural riddles whose key is buried somewhere in the remote phylogeny of the hibernants. We can recognize and describe this demi-death, but its basic function — and the mysterious factors that trigger it — eludes us just as surely as the hibernants elude winter.

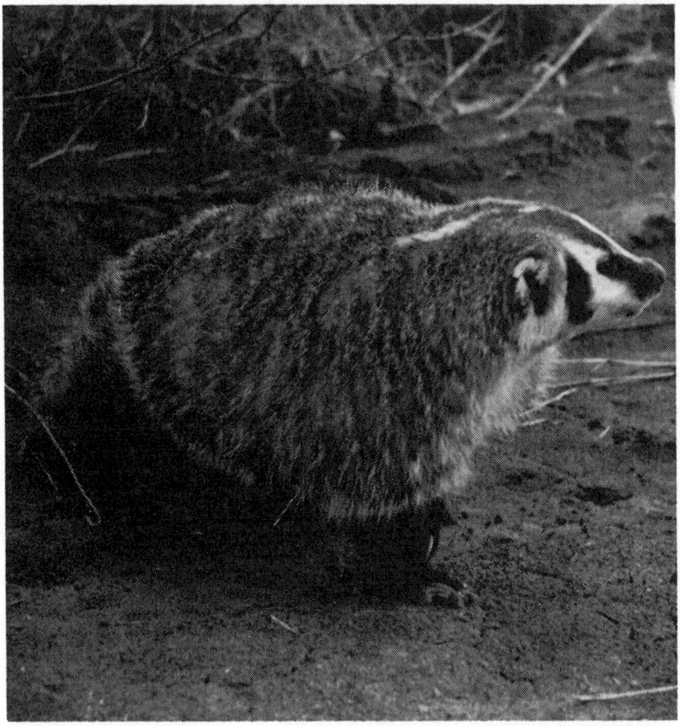

the fighting doormat

WHEN OLD SKIP, our favorite feist dog, began hollering his head off on the other side of the pasture hill, we didn't pay much mind. Skip was always raising something and then telling the world about it. But this time his barking was punctuated by a noise like a busted steam valve, so we trotted over for a look.

There was Skip, hackles up and giving ground a foot at a time. Coming up the hill at him was the steam valve noise — a hissing, grizzled engine of cussedness with a striped head as broad as my two hands — a big boar badger. He'd been cut off from his den but he was going home, dog or no dog, and he just bluffed Skip up the hillside and went to ground with a swagger.

Which doesn't say much for Skip's fighting blood, but a lot for his common sense. That badger, weighing twenty-five pounds or more, could have eaten his way right through the small dog. Squat, broad and powerful, with heavy muscles in back and shoulders to protect vital nerves and arteries, and with a loose, tough skin that he could almost turn within, he was designed for war.

Skip lived for fifteen years, and never tangling with badgers was one of the reasons. You hear some strong stories about dogs whipping badgers, but most of the farm dogs I've known have either given up or died trying. Badgers can strike almost too fast for the eye to follow, and their inch-and-a-half claws can disembowel a dog with one swipe.

Many years ago there used to be a Saturday night thing back home called "badger baiting," a perverted sport something like cockfighting. It consisted of putting a big badger in a barrel and sending some luckless dog in to pull him out.

There's a story told of a man who turned up with an alley cur he'd found somewhere, paid his entry fee, and entered the dog in the contest. The local bully boys were still winking slyly at each other when the stranger pitched the little mongrel into the barrel tail-first. The dog came howling out of the barrel with badger swarming all over him, dislodged the badger against a wall, and tore off down the alley. The bully boys were put out about it, but the stranger pocketed the money and strolled off into the darkness.

Of the American weasels, only the wolverine is larger than the badger. I've never seen a wolverine in action, but I'll vouch for the badger. Like all weasels he has immense vitality, seldom courting trouble but never turning it down when it comes calling. If it happens to be man trouble, he may not hesitate to attack.

My friend Frankie Heidelbauer was running his trapline one winter morning in northwest Iowa when he approached a set and found a newly-dug crater five feet across and two feet deep. When Frank stepped to the edge of the hole the badger came out swinging and took a swipe at the trapper's booted leg. He summarily shot the raging animal and was loading it into the packbasket when he noticed a tuft of red on one of the animal's claws. It was a bit of wool from a boot sock. The badger's claw had sliced through Frank's leather boot and into the stocking beneath without breaking the skin.

Old John Stopsack tells about trying to break up a badger party one evening on the top of Ocheyedan Mound in northwest Iowa. According to John, the courting badgers were kicking up such a fuss that no one could sleep. He went to the top of the great prairie rise with a hickory stave in his hand and fire in his eye, determined to give those badgers what-for. They gave it to John, instead, and ran him off the summit of Iowa's highest hill.

John tells this story in a very intense way, ending with: "And let me tell you, boy. . . don't you *never* try to whup badgers with a stick! They'll chaw it up and spit the splinters at you!"

But there are a few men who can handle badgers. Iowa Conservation Officer Roy Downing is one of them, and when the Iowa State Fair ends each fall the game wardens on duty at the fish and game building gather around to watch Roy round up badgers with his bare hands.

When Roy opens the door of a badger cage the huge weasel backs off into a corner, flattened and ready. If you've ever seen a steel spring waiting to unwind, it's a ready badger.

While the wardens make bets involving Roy's fingers, he reaches slowly in and makes deft feints. The hissing badger tolerates this for just so long and then strikes. In a blur of motion, Roy's other hand seizes a fistful of loose hide at the back of the animal's neck and he coolly withdraws thirty pounds of raging badger as if he were handling a puppy.

Like most wild hunters, the badger is very strong. The ropes and bands of muscle in back and shoulders are capable of enormous tetanus and endurance. I've seen a timber wolf shear a birch broom handle with one stroke, and a hundred-pound muzzled bear cub knock three powerful game wardens about. But my laurels go to the old boar badger that tried to tear up a semi-trailer truck.

The front bars of the badger cage of the Iowa Conservation Commission's traveling exhibit are made of five-sixteenths inch steel rods spaced at two-inch intervals. They are welded at top and bottom. One night a caged badger broke the weld on one of these, bent the rod up, and went to work on the next one. When the officer in charge pried the bar back into place the badger simply broke it off. The disgusted man closed the outside cage cover and went home.

During the night the badger attacked the expanded steel flooring of the cage, which is welded on all sides. He tore up one of these welds and opened up a six-inch hole in the cage floor. In despair, the exhibit officer turned the crusty old devil loose and replaced him with a younger, more reasonable animal.

Badgers are fossorial, or digging, animals. They are built for moving large quantities of real estate rapidly, and when they *really* dig they do so with all four feet and even their teeth, literally sinking out of sight. A dedicated badger can send a geyser of dirt shooting four feet into the air and can dig through hard sod and be completely buried — with the tunnel plugged after him — in less than a minute and a half.

Clyde Updegraff, late chief of Iowa's Boone Game Farm, once told me of a female badger that escaped from a cage and began a tunnel in a nearby pasture. Clyde and two of his helpers took after her with shovels and when they first began digging they could see her rump in the hole ahead. But that was the last time they saw her. The three men, digging most of an afternoon, never caught up with that badger.

Updegraff once put a big badger into a new pen with concrete flooring that had been poured the day before. The cement had not cured, but a man could safely walk on it. Yet, the badger dug down through fifteen inches of the green concrete, through the fox wire netting beneath it, and escaped!

Badger diggings may be distinguished from those of other animals because they are often vertical, from one to three feet deep, and look as if a major tunnel had been started and then abandoned. These are usually "prospect holes" dug in search of food, and are not uncompleted dens. For every home den the badger digs, he may dig hundreds of these pits. If he kills a larger animal such as a jackrabbit, he may even dig a special hole to eat it in.

He digs for nearly all his food — ground squirrels, gophers, prairie dogs, chipmunks, rabbits — and has the uncanny gift of knowing just about where in a burrow his next meal may be, and seems to be able to dig directly to it. Coyotes recognize this ability and it isn't unusual for a coyote to attach himself to a badger and follow him during a hunt. If a prairie dog or ground squirrel happens to slip away from the digging badger, Father Coyote can take it easily on open ground.

I once watched a hunting badger as he leisurely dug a series of prospect holes in a prairie pasture shortly after dawn. He proceeded with infinite patience in the stolid, unruffled manner of an old badger with the rising sun on his back. But in the midst of the project he suddenly popped out of a hole, ran to a place about ten feet away and began digging furiously, the dirt spouting up behind him. He caught something there (I was never sure what, although I looked the place over later) and then ambled easily around the shoulder of a hill, still hunting.

In his lifetime an old badger may dig literally miles of tunnels. He prefers bare, rolling hills and is almost never found in swampy areas or in heavy timber. He particularly likes to dig in sandy or gravelly soil where most burrowing animals hang out, and this has gotten him into trouble in some parts of the country where badgers have been accused of being ghouls. Years ago one badger was trapped in an

Ohio cemetery and exhibited as the "Wood County Grave Robber." He wasn't a ghoul, of course. He was a victim of circumstantial evidence, all because early settlers often established cemeteries on sandy ridges that were not good farmland — well-drained hunting grounds on which native badgers had prior claim.

The badger is death with a sense of humor — a clown by day and a skilled killer by night. In captivity he can be a shameless cornball and when the mood strikes him he may sprawl, flop loosely, or ball-up and watch you from between his hind legs. His doormat look is the result of very short legs and very long hair which may measure three inches on his sides but only half that length on his back. In the days when the best badger hair was used for shaving brushes, a prime pelt brought as much as $25. But the value of the fur has dropped in recent years. Today a pelt may bring only fifty cents. The price of badger fur was shaved by the electric razor.

This is to the benefit of us both, for the badger has always been one of my favorite critters. Maybe it's because we have tastes in common and prefer the same sort of country, for we both like to prowl grasslands that have never felt the breaking-plow, loafing in fields of blazingstar and rattlesnake-master with the summer sun on our backs.

But mostly, I think, my affection for old *Taxus* is directed at the fearless, confident way in which he carries himself. Especially when he's poking along a windswept hilltop in the depths of the prairie winter — ready for a feast, a fight or a frolic, and capable of handling any or all.

than a barrel of monkeys

A TRIBE OF ACCOMPLISHED killers, most of the weasel clan take life seriously. There isn't much slapstick in the daily doings of a mink, ferret or wolverine, and if a skunk has any light moments, no one much cares.

Yet, the biggest weasel on the upper river is an unabashed clown. This is the rare and beautiful river otter, a masterwork of aquatic design with the philosophy of a Groucho Marx.

It's a boldly-made animal, sometimes measuring over four feet long and weighing twenty-five pounds. But for all its size, you'll probably never see a river otter — that is a sight usually reserved for solitary trappers and rivermen. Of all the rare and secret creatures along the northern Mississippi, none are shyer and more sensitive to human intrusion. In over forty years on and around the Upper Mississippi, George Kaufman — Iowa's senior conservation officer — has seen only a few. In fact, otters are so seldom seen that they were once thought to be extinct along the upper river. But a few still hunt in the wild sloughs and islands, although no one is sure whether they are remnants of the original population or recruits that have drifted down into vacant habitat from northern Wisconsin and Minnesota.

Joe Martelle has seen several, and has even raced one through a remote slough.

Come winter, Joe strings his mink and muskrat traps for miles among the islands above and below the channel dam at Lynxville, Wisconsin. After the freeze-up his favorite mode of transportation — whether he's running his trapline or heading up to Lansing to see a movie — is on ice skates.

Joe was skating over his trapline one bright, cold day when he sighted a big male otter beneath the clear river ice. Skating just behind the otter, Joe followed it as the animal shot along under the ice. It wasn't a one-sided race, for an otter can travel a quarter of a mile under water and even out-maneuver some fish.

"Why, I could see that old cuss just as plain as anything," Joe told me. "He was every bit of four foot long and we had us a pretty good race, that otter and me. After a while he went his way and I went mine."

Joe is the only riverman I know who has seen an untrapped otter at such close range. You'll hear a lot of otter stories along the river, but most of them are tavern talk. A few otters have been taken in fishermen's nets and beaver traps along the Upper Mississippi, but such catches are as rare as they are unlawful.

I've never seen an otter on the upper river, and I doubt if I ever will. Twice I have seen wild otters — once on the Upper Jordan in Michigan and again near the headwaters of the Bois Brule — but that doesn't count. The nearest I've come to seeing a Mississippi River otter was the tail fins of some freshly-devoured shad on a mudbar that was laced with the big, web-footed prints of *Lutra*.

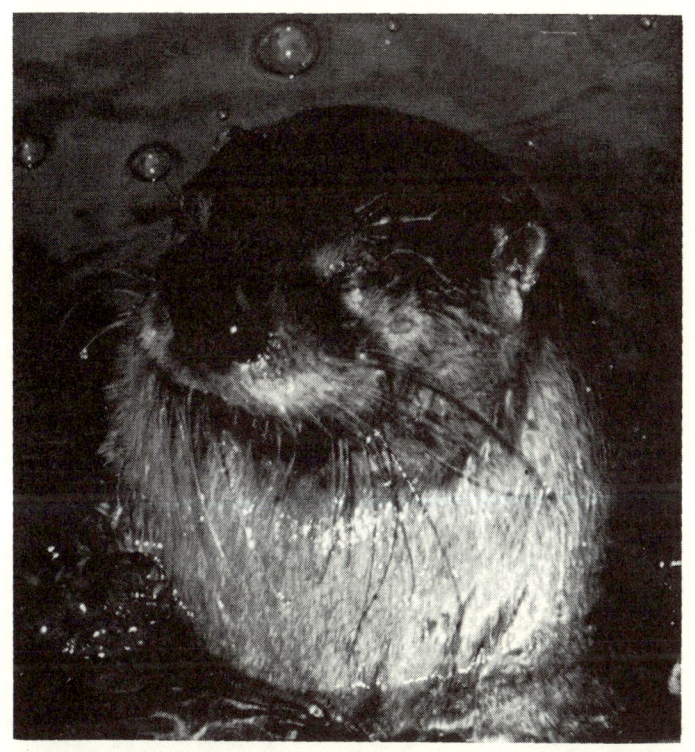

Whimsical, fun-loving and playful, the river otter is one of our most appealing wild mammals but — unfortunately — is very rare in most areas.

What I'm hoping for is to come drifting around the bend of some hidden slough some day and surprise a family of otters while they're sliding down a choice mudbank.

For nothing shakes an otter up quite so much as a steep mudbank and a little spare time. He climbs the bank and, with all four legs pointing backward, comes swooshing into the water. Whole otter families may join the fun, their wet bodies making the slide even slicker. When the stream is sealed by winter, they'll take to steep snow-covered hillsides like a troop of kids with Christmas sleds.

Although most weasels are morose and solitary, the otter loves company most of the year and is usually found in family groups. They may slide together for hours, or loll in the sun and take turns combing each other's dark, thick fur, "talking" lovingly in low mumbles. They often tumble and wrestle like children, and an old mother otter has been seen playing with a flat stone for hours, tossing it from paw to paw until she grew bored. Then she threw the stone into the water, dived for it, and apparently caught it in her teeth before it struck bottom.

With their long, scull-oar tails and webbed feet, otters are remarkable swimmers. They are also strong travelers and may range along nearly a hundred miles of riverbank in the course of a year, alternately swimming and moving over dry land.

Since their legs are so short, otters aren't very fast on their feet, although they can outrun a man for a short distance.

Once out of the water, an otter can't abide being wet and quickly dries itself by combing its fur and rolling in dry grass or leaves.

The otter that I sighted near the Bois Brule was about three hundred yards away, crossing a wet meadow toward a sluggish creek. I tried vainly to close the gap and get a better look at him but his clumsy, humping lope was faster than it appeared to be — much too fast for a jaded fisherman in hip boots.

If taken young, before they're set in their wild ways, otters can be psychologically "imprinted" by a human captor and make splendid pets. Emil Liers of Homer, Minnesota, has become famous with his pack of tame otters. He has even taught some of them to retrieve ducks on hunting trips and the animals follow him like low slung, whiskery puppies.

One day a few years ago, when Dr. Paul Errington and I were scrounging in the mudflats of Little Wall Lake for antique shotgun shells, the subject of otters came up. Paul told me that Liers had called him up one day when the Otter Man happened to be going through town. Liers wanted to know if there was some place nearby where he could exercise one of his pets — a good watercourse with no dogs around.

Errington and Liers took the otter out to nearby Onion Creek for an afternoon's workout. The otter humped happily along a mile of stream, turning over rocks and hunting crayfish and swimming in small pools.

"He was just as much at home under the water as above it," Paul said. "He was a beautiful animal. He was perfectly gentle, and when Emil whistled to him the otter would return like a dog."

When it was time to leave, the otter stumped up the creek bank on its absurdly short legs, rolled in the grass to dry its thick fur (otters can't abide being wet out of water) and followed Liers docilely back to the car.

Pet otters become warmly attached to their masters, and even to their masters' dogs. Liers was once walking through a field with his dog and several pet otters when a farmer's dog attacked Liers' Airedale. The otters joined the battle at once and drove the strange dog from the field. Another time, in Liers' own yard, he was savagely attacked and badly bitten by a strange dog. Several of his pet otters who were nearby rushed to his defense and roundly clobbered the dog. Such victories aren't surprising. One otter can handle a good-sized dog and several of them must be pure poison for any dog that steps out of line.

I envy Liers his otters. Ordinarily, wild pets don't stir me much for I've yet to see a wild animal that was enhanced in any way by captivity. But otters are somehow different, and Emil Liers has something there.

Not that I ever hope to keep an otter; I'll be lucky to just see one sliding in the sun down some Mississippi mudbank. That will be enough. What could I ever offer an otter that he doesn't already have in the Bunker Chute or Jughandle Slough?

A powerful and tireless swimmer, the otter is as much at home in water as on land. Its feet are webbed, and its broad tail serves as a sculling oar. Several swimming otters, diving and playing in single file, resemble a large sea serpent and may have originated legends about some land-locked "sea serpents."

geomys

UNDERGROUND, IN THE dark cool world of roots, grubs and earthworms, lives the Digger.

He is dedicated — heart, tooth and nail — to tunnelling. He is king of the miners, this "pocket gopher," and while a badger can dig faster he can't match the gopher's tireless capacity for drilling through real estate. One gopher dug three hundred feet in a single night. This might compare with a 150-pound man digging a trench seventeen inches wide and deep and seven miles long in ten hours.

You've probably never seen a pocket gopher. Like the mole, he's known less for his person than for his works — the fan-shaped mounds of fresh earth that appear in hayfields, pastures and roadsides where the Digger has pushed his loose excavate up to the surface.

He doesn't like to be above-ground. When he is topside the Digger is nervous and uneasy, moving in a small area with swiftness and economy of motion. He feeds or gathers nest material swiftly, cutting vegetation and stuffing it into the cheek pouches that named him.

The pocket gopher's scientific name, *Geomys bursarius,* literally means "earth mouse with pockets." Unlike most rodents, his facial pouches are true pockets and not just loose cheeks. They are lined with fur and open to the inside of the mouth through small slits near the lower jaw. Surprisingly capacious, these extend from the cheeks back along the neck to the shoulders, and are never used to carry dirt but only food and nesting material.

With his front feet the gopher stuffs cut grass first into one cheek pocket and then the other. He can pack away enough food for a full meal in half a minute. Then he pops back into his tunnel and slams the door behind him, a neat trick accomplished by shoving a bit of loose soil into place for an entrance plug.

Once sealed inside, he drops down a foot or two into a horizontal feeding tunnel, part of a burrow complex that may include a half-mile of winding, twisting passages. Here and there along these feeding tunnels are small pantries or food chambers packed with all sorts of trash — moldy roots, withering grass and other stale food items that the Digger couldn't resist bringing home, but which he's never quite gotten around to using.

Somewhere in this maze of feeding tunnels is another downward shaft that leads to the Digger's private chambers. The master bedroom may be as much as eleven feet beneath the earth's surface, and although a few tunnels wander off from this chamber, they are not as extensive as the food tunnels above.

Even in this nesting chamber the pocket gopher packs food and finely-cut grass. If it begins to spoil and becomes too much for him, he simply moves to another chamber. But if the Digger isn't neat, he is always clean and sometimes even has latrines along his passageways — small pits that are periodically covered and abandoned.

When a gopher gets a yen for fresh provender, he goes upstairs to the end of a feeding tunnel and begins to ex-

An unusual photo, demonstrating the pocket gopher's method of pushing excavated soil up to the earth's surface with his forefeet and nose. Taken in a glass-walled terrarium.

tend it. He works with his heavy front claws, loosening dirt and shoving it back between his front legs, beneath his body, and out behind him. During his mining his eyes are tightly closed and the lids permit no soil particles to get into his eyes. Even his ears are valved to prevent the entry of dirt. If the soil is hard and dry, he may use his great yellow incisors to loosen it, for like the beaver his lips can be closed behind the front teeth to keep dirt out of his mouth.

When a quantity of loose soil has accumulated behind him, the gopher pokes his head between his front legs, back between his hind legs, and twists at the same time. With a deft flip he is then facing the other way in his tight tunnel. Lying on his belly, he places his front feet, claws upward, in front of his face. Then he drives forward with his hind legs, a miniature bulldozer pushing the loose dirt before it. When there is more dirt than he cares to handle, he digs a short tunnel to the upper world and *voila!* — a gopher mound on your lawn.

If you happen to be sitting quietly nearby when this happens, you may get a rare look at the Digger.

He isn't very pretty. His eyes and ears don't amount to much, and his face is mostly yellow buck teeth. His front feet are armed with sets of long, heavy claws — the tools of his trade. Our plains pocket gopher is big as gophers go; from the blunt nose to the base of his hairless tail he may measure nine inches, with the tail adding another four inches. Although he's a clean animal, his short, velvet-soft fur tends to be the color of the earth in which he lives. In Illinois and Iowa he is almost black; farther west he becomes lighter and sandier in color.

Except during the mating season, pocket gophers are lone hands. They are vicious and will readily fight a man, dog or other gophers and if two of them happen to meet in a tunnel they may battle to the death. With the first spring rains, the Digger may throw caution to the wind and even travel overland in broad daylight. He is seeking a mate, who hides coyly in her tunnel waiting for her beady-eyed Galahad to show up. These wandering males may turn up almost anywhere at that time of year. I still have a scar on my left forefinger from such a gopher, who took a dim view of my eight-year-old hand trying to rescue him from a basement window-well.

Since it isn't too easy for gophers to get together, the mating season may be as much as three months long; if it were only a week or so, there wouldn't be many gophers.

There is a wide variation in litter size, which may range from one to nine young, and the birth of these baby gophers is one of nature's strangest miracles.

During birth, all baby mammals pass through the circular opening formed by the fusion of various bones in the pelvic girdle. In tunnel-dwellers such as the gopher, however, these bones are compacted and reduced to enable the animals to maneuver easily in their snug burrows. As a result, the pelvic girdle of the pocket gopher is quite constricted and Dr. Lloyd Ingles, a California zoologist, reports that the pelvic structure of a young female gopher is too compact to permit birth. However, during her first pregnancy, a hormone in the blood simply dissolves much, or most, of the pubic bones. So young gophers can be born without difficulty, in spite of their mothers' narrow hips!

Every maligned creature has some attributes. In the pocket gopher's defense, he aerates and mixes the soil with his tunnelling, and provides entry for moisture. By cramming some of his tunnels with neglected food, he provides subsurface organic material which enriches the soil with its decay.

Ge=mys shows himself in a rare appearance above-ground. He will probably carry the succulent twig below ground and store it in one of his many pantries. Uneasy above the surface of the earth, he is seldom seen.

But if the gopher is a miner by instinct, he's a sharecropper by profession. While his human landlords cultivate crops above-ground, the Digger harvests them neatly from below. A gopher can wreak havoc in orchards and gardens, and may extend a tunnel down a row of potatoes, wipe out every hill, turn at the end and work back up the next row. Young orchard trees are often killed by root-gnawing, and pasture and hayfield losses may run as high as ten percent of the crop.

There are ways of scragging such problem gophers, but it may take some doing. Patented gas pellets, poisoned baits or speartraps — complete with detailed instructions and money-back guarantees — sometimes get the job done.

Don't count on them, though. Your best bet will probably be a small farm boy who has a rusty trap and needs a dime.

fawns

GOBLINS AND ELVES have lost ground in most of today's forests.

The electric light and the picture tube have frightened them all away, driving them back into the few wild shadows that survive in such places as the Okefenokee and beneath the puncheon stoops of Ozark border cabins where wrinkled grannies still tell the old jump stories.

There remain among us, however, certain wood sprites that defy exorcism. Not only have they survived Science — something that elves could never do — but they are often sustained by Science, partly because they have succeeded in enchanting the Scientists themselves.

One cannot resist these sprites, and even the most case-hardened wildlife biologist catches his breath and hushes his footfalls at the sight of them. To such a man the white-tailed deer may be only *Odecoileus virginianus*, an even-toed ruminant of the family *Cervidae* in the great order of artiodactylids. But show that same biologist a white-tailed deer fawn asleep in its sumac nursery and he sees a wood sprite, just as the rest of us.

There is a quality that all wild animals have and never lose, and which deer have to the largest degree and their fawns most of all.

Nothing else in nature displays such mystic gentleness and utter delicacy of mood and form. The only way to describe such a fawn is to say that it should be set to music, with maybe some brisk country chords by mouth-harp and five-string banjo in the foreground — sort of jigging along through "Old Dan Tucker" or something — and backed by a tide of wistful, half-heard strings in full orchestra, swelling among the trees.

White-tailed fawn resting in a patch of May apple leaves.

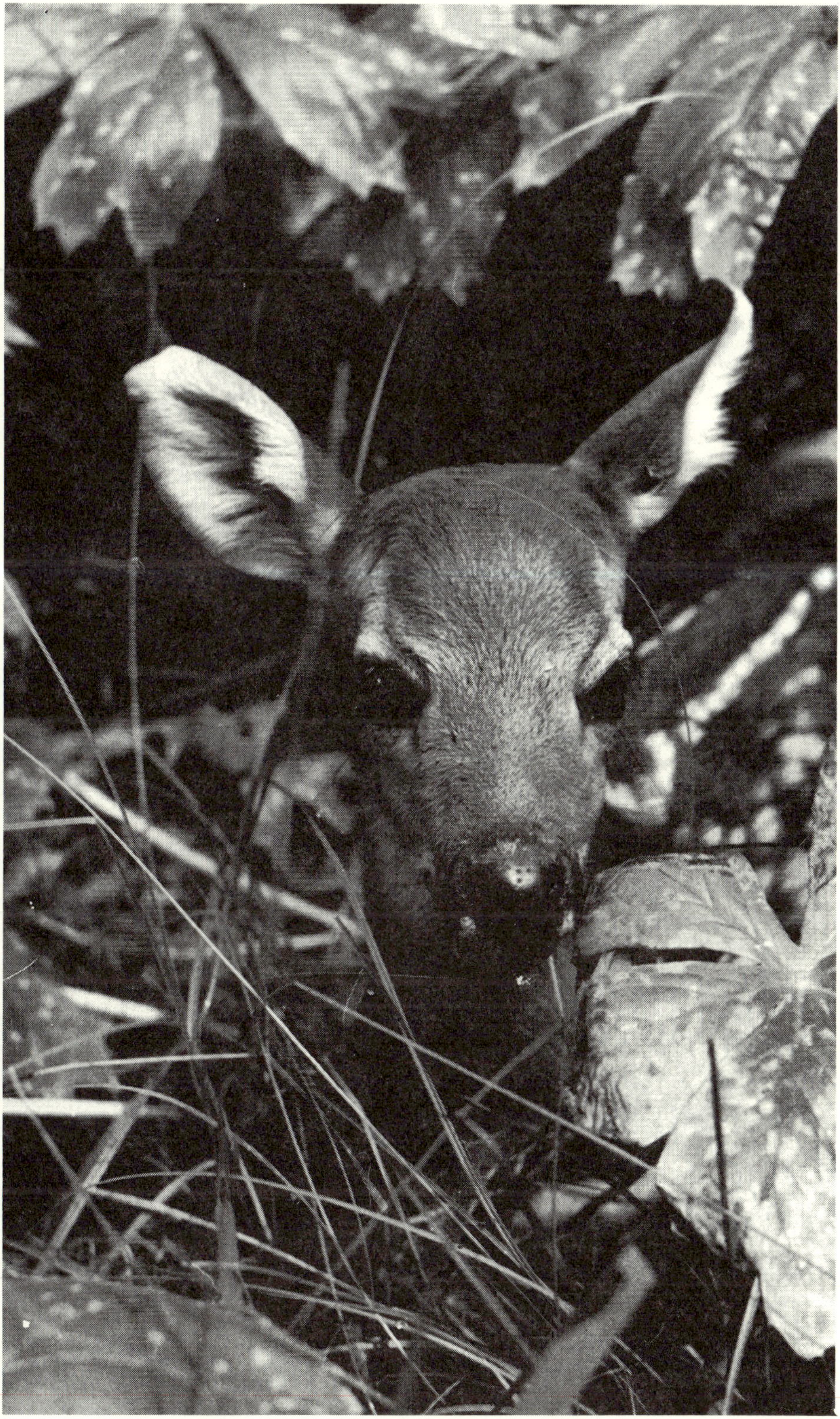

the river

old man river's shell game

WHEN JOE MARTELLE stepped out of his cabin door the night mists were still hanging over Harper's Slough and the first rays of the sun were just slanting in over the limestone bluffs on the Wisconsin side of the river.

It was not quite five in the morning but already a couple of johnboats were on the Mississippi, their big outboards driving them down the running sloughs to the clam beds. Downriver a flock of egrets rose from Jug Handle Slough and swung north over the timbered islands, and a pair of otters in Japan Slough lifted their heads and heard the coming of the distant boats.

Martelle pulled on his patched hip boots and walked stiffly down the steep bank to the 16-foot cedar johnboat with its pair of racked crowfoot bars. There'd been some rain up in Minnesota, he saw, and the river had risen an inch during the night. A good current in the big sloughs today, where a boat could drift right along but not too fast. This might be the day when a good man with a proper outfit could take a half-ton of shell, and maybe even find the pearl that would set him up for the rest of the summer. He put his lunch of beef, bread and water under the transom seat of the jo'boat, checked the gas in the auxiliary tank, and pushed off. The work day of the clammer had begun.

* * * * *

In the bed of the Upper Mississippi, half-buried in mud and silt, are scattered congregations of fresh-water clams. They are simple creatures, little more than two strong shells enclosing a soft, formless body. Blind and brainless, they lie on the river bottom with shells agape, laved in the currents that bring them food and oxygen.

Within each shell, partly surrounding the body, is a delicate mantle of tissue. This is the organ that builds the shell — rough and dark on the outside but with inner layers of pure, iridescent pearl. Three generations of fishermen on the upper river made their livings from this shell, shipping it to downriver factories for a nation's shirt buttons and cuff links. That was yesterday. Most of the shell is gone now and the fleets of fishermen have headed back to the farms or downriver to new industries. Only a handful of the old-time clam fishermen remains, a last-ditch defense against the zipper and the plastic button.

Joe Martelle is one of these rivermen, a small dark man with a French name whose people have been on the river longer than anyone can remember; blood kin to the old *couriers du bois* who set up the fur post of Prairie du Chien. He headquarters in Harper's Ferry, a little Iowa town across the river from Wisconsin and a few miles downstream from Minnesota. During the clam season from early June until late fall he's on the river whenever it's right for clamming, working the running sloughs for "washboards," "3-ridges," and the valuable little "ladyfingers."

The tools of his trade are simple, scarcely changed from the primitive gear of sixty years ago. The basic equipment is the crowfoot bar, a pole about twelve feet long that is festooned with short lengths of chain. From each chain is hung a pair of "crows' feet" — small, four-pronged grapnel hooks made of heavy wire. The boat drifts with the current and drags the crowfoot bar and its hooks along the river bed.

Feeding clams are sensitive to disturbance and will clamp tightly if touched by a foreign object. According to Hollywood, divers in tropical seas dread the great marine clams that can close on a swimmer's foot and drown him far beneath the surface of a lagoon. This same trait keeps the Mississippi clammer in business.

As a crow's foot passes over a gaping clam, the irritated bivalve seizes the wire hook with a viselike grip. When some instinct tells the fisherman that he's floated far enough over a clam bed, the crowfoot bar and its clam-encrusted hooks are heaved up into the boat and picked.

Martelle carries two crowfoot bars but works only one at a time to prevent fouling. They are handhewn birch poles cut from the rocky hillsides above the river; he scorns poles of metal or kiln-dried wood.

"No spring! My poles — look at 'em! Best on the river. They got spring, and the weight of the river just shapes them to the bottom so those hooks get down and work in the little holes. Most bars are too stiff and dead, with no give."

When Joe reaches the head of a likely-looking slough he cuts his power, "harnesses the mule," and begins his drift. The "mule" is a crude kite made of wood, sheet metal or anything else at hand, and floats before the boat attached to the bow with a rope harness. By making minute adjustments in the harness, the fisherman can deflect the river current at various angles and steer the drifting boat where he wishes. A cunning old river trick — steerage without power.

With the mule out, one of the crowfoot bars is dropped over the side and allowed to sink to the bottom, suspended by a rope bridle in twenty feet of brown water. Whenever Joe begins fishing, in spite of cold or rain, he's likely to take off his coat. I asked him about this one day.

"Lots of hooks on that bar," he replied, "and a lot of heavy chain. Now what if I was out here alone and snagged my coat when I put that bar in the river?"

Joe's been on the Mississippi a long time. I looked at the ranks of shiny, sand-scoured hooks and took off my jacket.

With the first crowfoot bar down, Joe can relax while his boat drifts a hundred yards or so. Then he raises the laden bar, hangs it temporarily on gunwale racks, and puts down the other bar.

Over a very good clam bed the clammer may raise a crowfoot bar every fifty yards, finding one or two mussels gripping every hook and sometimes even the chains. There may be eighty big clams on the rig and the fisherman must swing over a hundred pounds of crowfoot bar and mollusks up onto the rack. Thirty years of this have turned Martelle into barbed wire and rawhide, and even in a world of hardened rivermen his endurance has become famous.

Like most solitary fishermen and trappers, Joe is either dammed up or in full flood. As he works over good beds of seven-inch "washboards" he grows happier as the bars grow heavier, and the talk flows bankfull.

"God-dog, but look at that shell! Big shell that runs

heavy. Give us a hand!" And he looks up grinning, the deep weather wrinkles fanning over his face.

On such days — and they are rare days even if you know him well — he keeps up an unending flow of talk about the river and its sloughs, clams and their pearls, birds and critters on the banks, and storms on the great pools. He may tell of the old river jungles of Muscatine and Camanche and Sabula; of knifings, brass knucks and fur thieves. He talks of bounty-hunting rattlesnakes in the limestone crevices of the high bluffs, and of the secret caves he has found. He'll speak of all the things on the river that surprise and teach a man, and as he talks he swings heavy crowfoot bars up into the boat and fills it to the gunwales with money shell.

Then, at the end of the clam bed, Joe will stable his mule, ship the crowfoot bars, start the motor and head back up the slough to begin another drift. This goes on from before sunrise to mid-afternoon. Finally, with nine hours of such work already behind him, he must return to his cabin and cook out the shell.

Just below his place on the bank of Harper's Slough is a wooden box bottomed with sheet iron and with a firepit beneath. He fills this tank with several hundred pounds of clams, adds a little water, and covers the tank with burlap to seal in the steam. He builds a fire beneath the tank and in a few hours the clams have been killed and relaxed and their meats fall out of the shells. It's cruel labor that can occupy a late afternoon and evening, and in the full heat of August the job can raise feverblisters on a bullhide boot.

With the meats removed, the shell is graded according to weight and value, sacked, and left trustingly on the riverbank for the buyer. For the best thick, commercial shell Joe receives about $40 a ton; for thinner shell he gets much less. On an exceptional day he may take a thousand pounds of shell of all kinds.

It isn't always that simple. Some of the shell is worthless and must be discarded, and some valuable varieties may be too small to keep and must be returned to the river. Then, too, there are the eternal snags of the Mississippi. When a crowfoot bar fouls an ancient, sunken tree or log, the clammer must pull loose and risk ruin of his motor. The snag may be raised bodily if it's a small one, or several crowsfeet or chains may be torn away, or the entire crowfoot bar lost.

Martelle hates snags; he has lost several of his revered crowfoot bars on them, and at best they interfere with his fishing. He's also galled by the knowledge that some of the finest remaining clam beds are in old sloughs choked with sunken stumps and trees. During low water Joe has pollywogged for clams there, wading chest-deep and groping for the mussels with his bare feet.

He was all worked up awhile back over talk of a build-it-yourself diving outfit.

"Nothing to it," he told me one night in Jim Williams' tavern. "All we'd need would be some sort of air pump and we could strip them old sloughs. I know some that ain't been touched in fifty years!"

"Wonderful," I said. "I can handle air pumps."

"Well," Joe said, "I figgered I'd handle the pump and you'd dive."

"No," I said.

And there it stands. Joe has too much sense and I have too few guts to casually dive into the Mississippi's dark sloughs, and maybe we've muffed a chance for something more than shell. In one of those sloughs that's guarded by heavy, tangled snags there may be a virgin clam bed that holds the big pearl that Joe has sought for nearly forty years.

For in the back of every clammer's mind, no matter how stolid and hard-headed he might be, there is always the dream of the great pearl.

One day while we were clamming on Big Swifty Slough, Joe straightened up and flashed that fine smile that he inherited from some *voyageur* ancestor and said:

"For the next two hours we ain't fishing for the shell; we're fishing for the big pearl. We're going to find it today, man!"

We didn't, but Joe's still hoping. A few men along the river have found superb sweetwater pearls, and in the heyday of the clamming industry a large gem could build a man a home, buy him some land, or pay for a six-month binge.

There was the night in 1907 when a Harper's Ferry bartender sent an urgent message across the Mississippi to Wisconsin. A clammer was in his saloon, sopping up dime whiskey and offering a fine pearl for sale. His price dropped with the level in his jug and he was finally asking less than $500.

The bartender's summons was for John Peacock, a Prairie du Chien pearl buyer, begging Peacock to come a-runnin' before the drunken fisherman was bilked of his find. While a dozen fishermen watched quietly from the bar and the whiskey talk died down, Peacock placed his jeweler's loup in his eye and made his first appraisal by lantern light. Next day he bought the pearl for $1,000.

"It was risky," he reflected recently. "Appraising that way by a coal-oil lamp, I mean. Oh, it wasn't the biggest pearl that had come my way, but it looked like the finest. When I saw it by daylight, I knew I'd been right. That pearl went to a Chicago dealer for $5,000, and eventually ended up in the New York market."

One of the few old-time Mississippi pearl buyers still alive, Peacock told me there had once been twenty-seven registered pearl buyers staying at the Prairie du Chien hotel — agents from India, France, England and all parts of the United States.

Sixty years ago, when the river boomed with clam fishermen, the buyers had breakneck horse races along the levees when word leaked out that a clammer had found a fine pearl while cooking his shell. Lucky fishermen were overwhelmed by the cash bids but usually managed to keep their perspective. Their wives were usually shattered. For the first time in their lives the women were within reach of new mohair sofas and homes of their own, and they didn't plan to let them slip by. There were several times when Peacock would have jacked up his offers to pearl owners but their near-hysterical wives just couldn't stand the gaff of bargaining.

Some finds were sheer, fantastic luck. A northern Iowa fisherman bought some clam meats — fine catfish bait — for use on his trotlines. He came home with his catch one afternoon, cleaned it, and threw the catfish offal to his chickens. As he sat smoking on his back stoop he noticed a scrawny rooster having trouble with one of the catfish innards and the man ambled over to investigate. In the section of catfish intestine, too big for the rooster to swallow, was a rough, discolored pearl. The fisherman saw Peacock a few days later and snapped up the pearl buyer's offer of $150.

Late that night, when his house was silent and he could concentrate on his delicate job, Peacock carefully peeled off the blemished outer layer of the pearl and revealed one of the rarest gems of his career — a pearl of deep, pigeon-blood red.

Color tones of fresh-water pearls depend on the mother shell. The big "washboard" clams usually have pink pearls, as do the "wavey-backs." The "3-ridges" have pearls in shades of blue, green and lavender, and the rare and valuable "niggerhead" clam has pearls of shifting blue and pink. From the "muckets" come fine pink pearls and the "sandshells" have pearls of salmon-pink. And from the delicate little "ladyfingers" come the most beautiful of all — the prized black pearls with slaty fires of blue and violet iridescence.

A pearl is built by the mollusk's mantle, the organ that deposits mother-of-pearl within the shell. When a small foreign particle cannot be ejected from a clam, the mollusk secretes raw pearl, or nacre, around the particle to soothe the irritation. This nacre is built up in layers, and a pearl can be peeled like an onion.

Most pearly concretions in fresh-water mussels are misshapen slugs, or "baroques," which may have some value as costume jewelry but not as gems. "Chickenfeed" is river jargon for the tiny seed pearls that are sold by the ounce, the current market standing at about $5. These were once in demand by Indian buyers for use on saris and the costumes of upper caste Asians.

The Mississippi pearl market was struck a deathblow by the Japanese cultured pearl. By creating gems in special beds under controlled conditions, the Japanese were able to supply good matched pearls and undercut the value of the rarer wild pearls. A necklace of 40-grain matched pearls may be had today for $500; it might have cost several thousand dollars fifty years ago.

Peacock considers cultured pearls high in quality despite their relatively low price, and despite his old love for river gems. At the same time he contends that fresh-water pearls can equal any produced in a Pacific lagoon, usually considered premium gems because of their exotic pedigree.

A lot of pearl fanciers take issue with this, holding that inland rivers lack many salts and minerals found in the ocean and that river gems are softer and duller than marine pearls. Yet there may always be a market for sweetwater pearls since most cultured gems run to whites and pinks. River pearls of black, red or violet may command a good price because of their rarity and the great difficulty of matching them.

But today's sweetwater pearl will no longer make a clammer rich, or buy him that six-month spree. A twenty-grain gem found a few years ago near Harper's Ferry brought only $120, a fourth of its value in 1910. Martelle has several small pearls and if they average $30 he'll consider himself lucky. Even so, he keeps them cached in a hidden poke, as much from habit as anything else. Old-time rivermen don't advertise the pearls they have on hand.

To yesterday's clammer, heavy shell was meat and potatoes and the rare perfect pearl was gravy — a hope and dream that helped build the clamming fleets. However, when the original clam beds began to dwindle, the promise of fine pearls faded with them.

There was a time, seventy years ago, when the great primeval clam beds paved miles of river bottom with millions of tons of shell. In 1891 a German button cutter named J. F. Boepple sired an era when he brought his Old World skills and tools to Muscatine, Iowa and set up the first button factory on the Upper Mississippi. As the factory flourished in the 1890's, others mushroomed along the river. A button tariff by President McKinley had created a high demand for domestic pearl buttons and Boepple once said that this tariff had made buttons so valuable that churchgoers had begun putting coins in the collection plates.

Whole families took to the river. Every summer large clamming camps sprang up in northeastern Iowa and in Wisconsin and Minnesota, and grocery packets plied the river selling supplies at swollen prices. Farmers complained as sons and hired men deserted farm drudgery for the color and noise and quick money of the clam camps. Riverfront saloons boomed and riverbanks were piled high with ripening clam meats. The wild islands became even wilder and some island camps were virtually beyond the law. Bearded, sun-blackened rivermen came upstream from Cape Girardeaux, and downstream from Lake Pepin and the Wisconsin pulp forests. They worked for a time, blew their shell money on roaring sprees, and disappeared. Often someone else's boat, or pearls, vanished with them.

The first of the clamming was at the factory door in the broad clam beds before Muscatine. More than 300 boats could be seen working over one productive mussel bed. In the winter these fishermen were joined until freezeup by sawmill workers, lumberjacks, and other seasonal laborers.

In 1896, five hundred tons of shell were taken from one clam bed two miles long and a quarter-mile wide. By 1898, a thousand full-time fishermen were working 167 miles of river between Fort Madison and Sabula, half-way up Iowa's eastern border. A bed one and one-half miles long near New Boston, Illinois, yielded ten thousand tons of shell in three years, a probable total of a hundred million clams. As the great beds near southeastern Iowa petered out, the fishing extended southward into Missouri and upriver to Wisconsin and Minnesota. In 1899 it was the most valuable commercial fishery in Wisconsin and over sixteen million pounds of shell were marketed.

No shellfish can withstand such immense fishing pressure.

and within a decade of the first button factory the great Muscatine beds began to fade. So did Lake Pepin in Minnesota, which produced four thousand tons of marketable shell in 1914 but only a hundred and fifty tons in 1929. By 1946, two Illinois biologists found no clam fishing below Muscatine at all, and even during ideal weather and river stages there were no more than a dozen clamming boats on the Muscatine waterfront. In Harper's Ferry there are less than five parttime clammers today.

Clams grow slowly and conditions must be right for their increase. Female clams discharge huge numbers of larvae, their *glochidia,* into the water and these tiny organisms must hitch a ride or die. Some encyst themselves in the gill filaments of specific fish, where they grow for a short time before leaving their hosts and falling to the river bottom. If the young clams survive, it may still be ten or fifteen years before they reach commercial size.

As eroding watersheds leached into the upper river, many of the famous old clam beds were buried by silt. While the uplands washed into the river, and pollution from growing cities added its venom, the heavy fishing pressure continued.

Attempts were made to save the mussels, of course. New laws were enacted to greatly curtail clamming. Hopefully, the U. S. Bureau of Fisheries set up a biological station at Fairport, Iowa, in 1908, and began artificial propagation of clams. Young clams were produced in vast numbers in darkened troughs and host fish such as sheepshead and buffalo were infected with the clam larvae and released. During only two months in 1920, rescue crews infected six million fish with nearly five hundred million glochidia.

It may have helped a little, but not enough to revive a dying industry. The old clam beds had been ravished faster than they could replenish themselves, and an era passed on the Upper Mississippi.

To an entire new generation the decades of the button

shell have never existed. It is a time slipping out of modern memory, and "crowfoot bar" is a term that stands strange and distant on the ear.

But here and there along the Mississippi, on the upper reaches of the river where it runs between limestone bluffs and sprawls among the wild islands, a few men are still at the job of clamming. They are the last of their breed — men who live apart from TV reception, suburbia, and other frantic trappings of our era. Their ways are built around their cedar johnboats, the sagging price of shell, and the strength of the river current.

Joe Martelle still gets up at first light and goes out on the bayous and hidden lakes just as he did thirty years ago, and as his people did before him. And someday, when they've had rain up in Minnesota and the current in Big Swifty Slough will drift a jo'boat steady but not too fast, maybe Joe will find his big pearl.

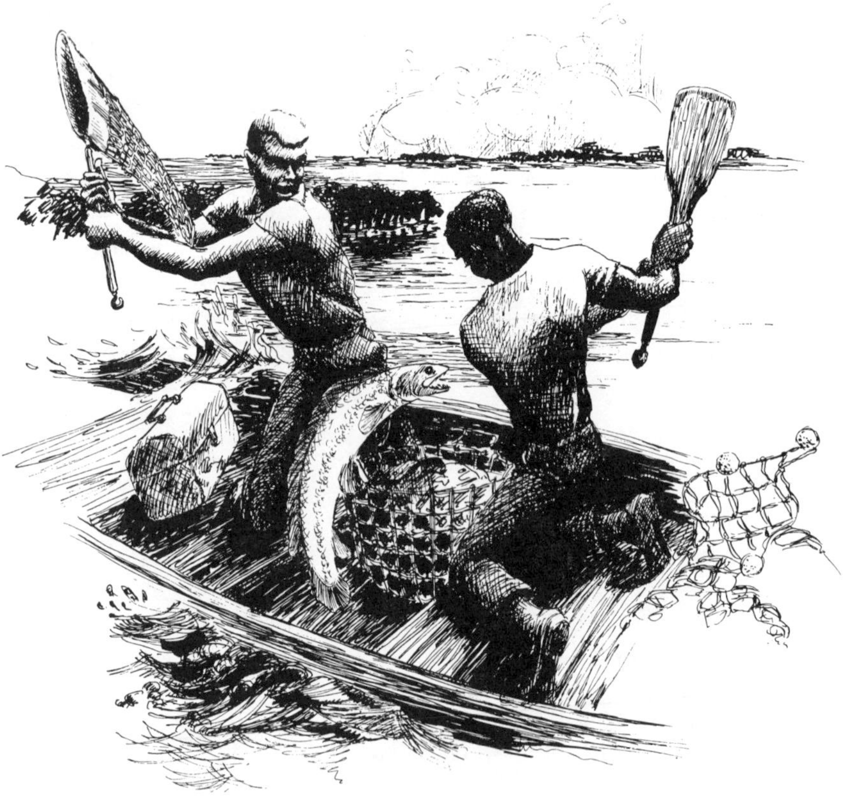

outlaw of the dark sloughs

JOHN A. GRINDLE is a stupid, vicious thug. About the only good things you can say about him are that he fights to the death, takes care of his family, and helps hold the status quo in the teeming Mississippi backwaters.

Depending on where he hails from, he may be called a mudfish, dogfish, bowfin, grindle cat, or just grindle. He's usually a "dogfish" to Yankees. Down south the boys call him "John A. Grindle" for reasons no one can remember.

He is a hangover from an ancient time, and like any hangover he is not pleasant to behold. His body is a heavy cylinder of muscle armored with tough cycloid scales, with a blunt, slightly flattened head that's split by a mouth studded with strong, sharp teeth. A low, long dorsal fin extending down the length of his back seems to have a will of its own, undulating and rippling, and capable of slowly moving the fish through the water without other body movements.

As close as John A. Grindle ever comes to being attractive is in the spring when he wears his courting colors. His lower fins become a vivid paint green and a dark spot on his tail is bordered with brilliant yellow. The long dorsal fin is dark green with a narrow olive band along the upper margin and near the base. The rest of the time he's just a dull olive above, with a conventional cream-colored belly.

I first met John Grindle while crappie fishing near a weedbed in Gun Barrel Slough, when he grabbed my bait minnow and took off for Memphis. He fought deeply with strong surges and behaved something like a northern pike. Even when he ran out of gas and was brought to the boat he was still trying to bite through the hook. One look at his dentition was enough to dampen any ideas of removing the hook by hand, so I just busted him with a gaff and cut the hook out. Even that took some doing. Old John doesn't give up the ghost easily, and rivermen tell of dogfish living all night on a riverbank. His swim bladder is a primitive lung, and he can gulp air and breathe after a fashion, much as the lungfishes. In cool weather, in the shade, he can live for twenty-four hours out of water.

He fights like a game fish, but unlike some big bass and pike he shows few resources. I've never had a bowfin fight toward a rock or snag in an attempt to break the line. He simply hauls away like a mad dog, with no finesse or strategy. In the dead, heavy heat of August a dogfish doesn't fight hard or long; there's usually just one strong flurry and he gives up. At that time of year he may be somnolent and flabby, but in cool water it's another story. The dogfish's muscles grow solid and when hooked he shows lasting power. In spring or fall a big dogfish can put up a vicious, prolonged battle that is the equal of any northern pike's the same size.

A couple of us were fishing one June evening near a boat landing in the Green Island Bottoms — a sort of cornbelt Everglades that lies beside the Mississippi halfway up Iowa's eastern border. It was coming on sundown when a stranger walked up, rigged some light casting tackle, and began working the shallows with a small weedless spoon.

Not far away three old gaffers were fishing for bluegills and getting a big belt out of the dude and his fancy tackle. The stranger ignored them and went about his business, casting capably out into a patch of flooded smartweed. He hadn't been at it long when there was a strong swirl in the brown water, a commotion in the vegetation, and the line went slack. The stranger coolly reeled in his line and bent on another lure.

The oldtimers took all of this in, winking and elbowing each other as oldtimers will when they've seen a dude bested.

"Say, mister," called one of the old gents. "Mebbee this here slough's short on bass, but it's mighty tall on grindles!"

The stranger grinned happily back over his shoulder and resumed casting.

"Sure hope so," he said.

That was the first purist bowfin fisherman I'd ever seen, a sportsman who made a specialty of catching dogfish. I've met several since, and in their own way they're just as dotty as trout fishermen.

The best way to fish for dogfish is to fish for something else. I've never caught one on purpose. Dogfish hit best when you don't want them to, usually while you're having some good bass fishing in spring. They'll attack almost anything in the water that appears reasonable to attack. They will strike any natural or artificial bait that moves, especially in spring when the males are guarding egg-filled nests in shallow weedbeds or watching over the newly-hatched bowfin larvae that cement their snouts to plant rootlets about the nest. Even after these dogfish fry are free-swimming, their male parent continues to guard and herd them, slashing out blindly at any real or imagined threat.

Few dogfish caught on hook and line weigh over eight

pounds. The real lunkers are usually taken in nets by commercial fishermen who tell of giants running nearly twenty pounds. These fish are often ones that have been marooned in overflow ponds or oxbow lakes. In such waters, cut off from the main river channel, fishermen may net a few huge dogfish and nothing else. All other fish have been eaten.

Something's always bothered me. Who was the original John A. Grindle? It's an old name and its owner — probably some old river rat — has been long dead. If he was anything like his namesake, it's just as well; he must have been meaner than an acre of snakes.

About ten years ago a federal fish hatchery's bass-rearing ponds on an island in the upper river were inundated by spring floods. The receding river left countless rough fish in these rearing ponds. There was nothing to do but kill everything and start all over.

So one morning we steeped the ponds with fish poison, dragging sacks of rotenone behind boats. It wasn't long before the "fine" fish began to roll in final agony on the pond's surface — walleye, pike, crappie, bass, sauger, sunfish, and silver bass. The coarse fish took longer, for gar and dogfish die hard.

We worked in teams, one man rowing and the other dipping up dead and dying fish. I stood in the bow of an 18-foot jo'boat with a large dipnet while Ed Vil, an entomologist from Haiti, handled the oars. Everything was going along fine until I dipped up a huge female dogfish that was wallowing weakly on the surface. The fish appeared to be almost dead, but when I dropped it into the boat it came to life, kicked its way out of the bin, and tried to take over the boat. The battle was joined.

All hell broke loose amidships. The dogfish was all over the place and so were I and the dipnet. There was a heavy steel eye on the end of that dipnet's handle and it was pretty rough on the cedar planking of the boat. As if that weren't

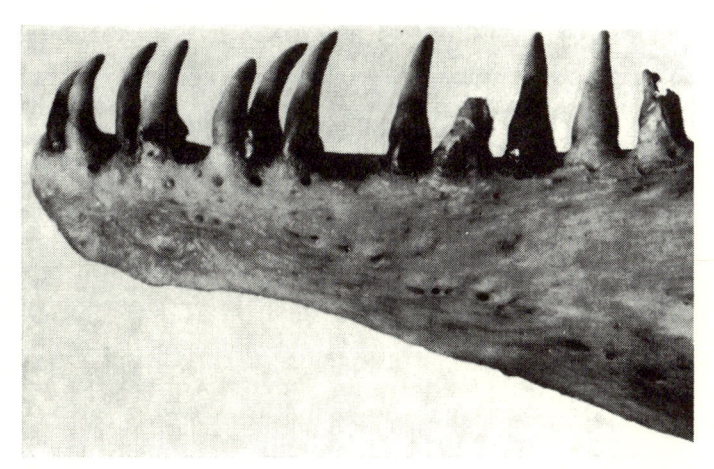

Enlarged photo of lower jaw of dogfish, showing strong, recurved teeth.

bad enough, Vil began roaring invective in Haitian French and cutting at the dogfish with his nine-foot pushpole.

Except for the gars, no fish in North America can soak up more punishment than dogfish, in water or out. They're big, strong, well-armored and mean. They have that trick swimbladder-lung, and in the past 190 million years they've developed the knack of survival.

Well, what with the thrashing dogfish, the slippery footing and the flailing dipnet and pushpole, Ed and I suffered almost as much as the fish. Scales, splinters and Haitian epithets flew and the fish seemed to take new strength each time it was clobbered.

The fight didn't last long, but it seemed like it. After a while we finally contained the enemy and beached the boat covered with blood, slime and glory. When the federal man in charge of the project saw his boat, he asked us if we'd mind staying ashore and not helping him anymore. That was very good of him, and Ed and I spent the rest of the afternoon in the shade, drinking icewater and telling voodoo yarns and watching everyone work in the hot sun.

Vil went home soon after that, and I haven't heard from him since. But sometimes when I'm on a dark, deadwater slough and see a shoal of minnows break water in terror, I think of dogfish and Ed Vil and hear a Calypso saga:

"*Oh, de great white shark what swim in de Carib-ee,*
Boss of de Carib-ee.
He de mightiest fish in the southern sea
But he all wropped up in his misery
For he don' got a name in history
Like ol' John Grindle of de Mississipp-ee!"

the world of charley gibbs

THE OLD BURNISHED richness of October was on the land, flavored with woodsmoke and tempered with frosty nights. That morning the western wall of the Mississippi's valley had blazed with color where the sun struck it, while the colors of the eastern shore were muted in shadow and the great valley buttresses stood somber, ranked far upstream into the hazes of Minnesota and Wisconsin.

By noon, when the last of the skin ice had melted from shaded pools, Charley Gibbs had already been on the river for nearly seven hours running his fyke nets and basket traps. It was a long time since breakfast when he pulled into a quiet slough just behind the Butterfly, lashed his loaded johnboat to a snag, and waded ashore where the willows were thinnest.

In ten minutes he had a driftwood fire roaring near the shore of the island. He went to the boat and took off his rubber apron, broke out a blackened dutch oven and a sack of provisions, and carefully selected a solid, big-scaled carp from the fish bin amidships. Returning to the fire, he set the kettle in place and dropped in a pound of lard. While the grease melted, he squatted beside a drift log and swiftly fleeced the scales from the carp with a thin-bladed knife, gutted and beheaded it, deeply scored the sides to expose the bundles of tiny faggot bones, and cut the fish into chunks.

When the lard was smoking, Gibbs dropped in the chunks of fish and turned to his grubsack again, taking out some potatoes and onions that he diced into the pot.

For fifteen minutes he sat on the driftwood log and regarded the dutch oven. Then he stood, head averted to escape the spatter, and poured in a half-gallon of water from the boat tin. He carefully arranged more driftwood about the steaming kettle, added a huge dollop of butter as an afterthought, and returned to the log to mournfully stare at the fire.

Forty minutes. He had just fed the fire again and added more salt to the kettle when a bent willow branch was released in the thicket somewhere behind him, and there was a faint scrape of canvas on wood. Without turning, Gibbs spoke.

"You're noisier than a herd of hawgs."

A short, weathered man in a faded hunting coat parted the screen of willows and scowled ferociously at Gibbs' back.

"You ornery old devil. You got something to eat? I'm hungry as hell."

"You been hungry fifty years. How come us poor working men always got to feed you game wardens?"

George Kaufman stepped up beside the sitting man and darkened the terrible scowl.

"Either I get some of that chowder or I'm gonna rassle you. I'd throw you in the river except it would poison the fish."

Gibbs rose wearily, looked at the bristling little warden with pained forbearance, and growled fondly:

"Reckon I'll feed you. You can't paddle that toy canoe home on an empty belly and I sure don't want you riding with me."

Fisherman Charley Gibbs heaves a heavy grapnel hook overboard to snag a net sunk in a Mississippi slough. He has lined up the spot by landmarks. He snagged the net on his second toss and emptied it of fish.

The smell from the dutch oven was enough to break a hungry man's heart. Lansing fish chowder, smoking hot, riding the wind for a half-mile to draw in a hungry game warden. There was a little more ritual cussing and routine blasphemy, but not much. Not even Three-Finger George can bristle and cuss when the chowder is ready, and it's October on the upper river. . . .

Charley Gibbs is an old hand at cooking fish chowder, and in capturing the ingredients. He is 53 years old, a spare, well-used man with a slightly horsy face that is often shaded with melancholy, and with that distant quality in and about the eyes that is usually found in old sailors, hunters and rivermen. He is a commercial fisherman — inland kin to the men who kill cod and tuna — and the third generation of his family to fish the Upper Mississippi. For over forty years Charley Gibbs has earned his living by catching fish and selling them.

In mid-spring and mid-autumn it is usually good work. But in March and November it can be a cruel trade and even a deadly one. Such as the November of 1940 when the Armistice Day blizzard killed dozens of duck hunters on the upper river and when some commercial fishermen — marooned on river islands by the subzero gale — burned boatloads of precious nets and seines to keep alive.

The Upper Mississippi is not a region of moderation. It's mostly too hot, too cold, or too windy. There's always too much of one thing and not enough of another. There are January days of thirty below when the thick ice booms and rumbles with the cold, when even the icebreaker *Fern* can't smash the white barriers of the upper river, and when the dripping nets of the winter fishermen turn to crystal wire as they are lifted out into the wind.

And then there are July and August when the river is hot to the touch, when the Lansing pool becomes a brass mirror of heat and the air is only a hundred degrees less than the boiling point and a man can hardly breathe on the island lakes where dense flood plain forest cuts off the wind. This is the storm season when tornadic winds may do their best to blow Old Man River out of his bed. The broad, open pools behind the channel dams are worse. Towboats caught in these summer squalls have their lower decks buried in brown water and their deck cabins flooded as ten-foot combers march aboard. In such winds a tow of barges and their 15,000 tons of cargo may be cracked like whips and driven into the bank or onto stump-filled shoals beside the channel.

But for all its violent moods, this stretch of the Mississippi is a rich fishing ground that teems with channel catfish, carp, buffalo fish, fresh-water drum, pike, bass and sturgeon.

Charley Gibbs' work world is a tangled river wilderness of channels and sloughs about six miles long and nearly three wide, the broad Lansing pool that lies above Channel Dam 9.

Like most commercial fishermen, Gibbs believes that somewhere in the river are the "fishes' sidewalks" — routes travelled by river fish during migrations and feeding movements. These pathways shift and fade with river levels and changes in bottom contours, and are bonanzas where fishermen using trammel nets and seines beneath the ice may take over seven tons of fish in a day.

Gibbs seldom fishes in winter; he uses that season to build new boats and repair his equipment. But he makes an all-out effort in early spring and late fall when there's floe ice on the river and carp and other "money fish" are bunched up. At such times, Gibbs will use trammel nets that trap fish in pockets of fine mesh. Two-thirds of his annual catch may be made in his spring and fall fishing; the bin in one of his boats holds a half-ton of fish and there have been many days when Charley has had to return to the dock and unload his catch with his nets only half-run. There have been other days when the fish bin in his boat has stayed empty.

In summer he may have as many as fifty hoopnets and forty basket traps in the river at once. A hoopnet is a long cylinder of coarse webbing that is held open by metal rings or hoops. There is a "throat" in the mouth of this net, a webbing funnel into which fish can swim easily but cannot escape. A fyke net is simply a large hoopnet with long fences of net leading to its mouth.

A basket trap is a wooden version of the hoopnet used to catch catfish and is baited with cheese scraps or maybe a female catfish to attract males during the spawning season. Basket traps are always anchored. But heavy as these waterlogged wooden traps may be, Gibbs has had them stolen by beavers that cut the anchor lines and tow the traps away to be built into dams.

In a shallow bayou, where low islands teem with wild game, Charley Gibbs hauls in a fyke net. In such water much of the catch may be game fish, but these are returned to the river unhurt. "We'd rather catch rough fish," Gibbs explains. "We don't like to catch game fish any more than the sportsmen like us to."

Hoopnets and fish baskets are placed by judgment and found by instinct. Gibbs never uses marker buoys or blazed trees on the shoreline to mark his fishing spots. His nets and traps may be sunk in two fathoms of featureless slough that is rimmed by a blank wall of willows. But Charley will gauge the shoreline with a narrowed eye, line up some mysterious checkpoints, and heave his grapnel hook into the river. Dragging it slowly over the riverbed, he accurately snags the short anchor rope of a fish trap. Up comes the muddy, dripping crate with its pounding cargo of catfish.

This is a premium catch. Streamlined and scaleless, with fleshy whiskers that named them, the channel catfish are some of the sweetest eating that swims in fresh water. Best of all are the "fiddlers" from fourteen to eighteen inches long — firm, delicate and in high demand.

Most shore folks never eat the best part of a catfish. In the heads of breeding catfish in spring, enlargements of muscle form behind and under the eyes. These catfish "cheeks" or "chops" are solid lumps of meat that are carefully cut out by many commercial fishermen. As large as the ball of a man's thumb, a catfish cheek is firm, white and succulent — something like a prime scallop. If a commercial fisherman troubles to cut out catfish cheeks, these Mississippi morsels won't find their way to the market. They go home with the fishermen.

Strange things swim in Charley Gibbs' world. There are the fresh-water drum or "sheepsheads," whose inner ears hold the lucky stones so prized by small boys in the river towns. There are the paddlefish — boneless, primordial hangovers with tails like sharks and noses flattened into long, broad paddles. They are found in only two places in the world — in China's Yangtze River, and in the Mississippi drainage where they beat slowly along river bottoms and feed in the ooze.

There are the little hacklebacked sand sturgeon, and the great black rock sturgeon that weigh as much as a man and can shred a hundred dollars' worth of gillnet as they roll and plunge in the mesh. There are also gars, voracious and predatory, sheathed in scales that were tough enough to face pioneer plowshares. There is old John A. Grindle — the bowfin, or dogfish — last surviving member of a family that swam with dinosaurs.

But one of the strangest is a giant minnow that is at once the curse and the blessing of the upper river.

This is the "German carp," a tough European immigrant that invaded the Mississippi in the early 1880's. Cultivated by the Chinese for centuries, raised by Romans in artificial ponds and finally brought to this country by optimistic experimenters, the carp is a prized fish in Europe. But in the New World it became a bully of the habitat, muddying the water in its incessant rooting about the bottom and literally crowding out game fish. Weighing up to fifty pounds, the carp shoulders other fish aside and smothers sensitive game fish populations with its immense reproductive capacity and an ability to dominate almost any freshwater habitat.

The first records of carp in the Mississippi were in 1883, and it was about then that the first one was caught near Lansing by Sever Olson. The small fish completely mystified Lansing rivermen until a German druggist identified it. "Doc" Nachtwey was so delighted to see a fish from back home that he paid Sever a dollar for it. This was the first dollar of millions to be paid for Mississippi carp. Within a few years there were carp everywhere in the upper river. A half-million pounds were caught in 1894, and by 1899 six times that many were taken. Carp are shipped in huge quantities to the eastern markets today, and although the "buglemouth bass" is cursed and despised by sport fishermen, it is the top money fish in the Mississippi.

Times have changed along the river, and fish and fishermen have changed with them. Sturgeon are fewer, and more highly prized. In the old days, rock sturgeon in the Upper

Mississippi were caught only for their roe which was drained, salted, packed and shipped to Russia to be labelled and exported to this country as Czarist caviar. But today rock sturgeon are painfully rare in the upper river and their smoked flesh brings top money.

The eel fishery has collapsed, largely because of the new channel dams that block upstream migration. Skipjack and some other migrants have also become rare in the upper river for the same reason, and paddlefish and buffalo fish have declined slightly as the habitat has changed and fishing pressure grows heavier.

There are changes among the men, too. Charley Gibbs no longer works a sixteen-hour day although he may be on the river for a solid twelve hours, and like all other commercial fishermen he now uses powerboats. Not many years ago all commercial fishermen rowed their johnboats. One mighty boatman — disgusted at the price of fish at New Albin, Iowa — once rowed his 3,000-pound cargo of fish eleven miles to Lansing only to find that the price was the same there.

Most fishermen also have replaced their linen and cotton webbing with rotproof nylon, even though some old-timers growl that nylon knots slip and nylon webbing sings in the current and warns fish.

One thing hasn't changed: there are still many jobs in which a man can earn higher wages than in commercial fishing, but few jobs today where a man can be more his own boss. The commercial fisherman operates under some checks and demands similar to those of the self-employed farmer, but is not afflicted by government controls, bureaucratic pingpong, and high land and equipment costs. Charley Gibbs pays about $200 each year in license fees and has nearly $20,000 invested in nets, boats, motors and other gear. In a good year he may take in $8,000 — a good income on the river — and is far less vulnerable to drought, crop loss and capital depreciation than the average farmer. On the other hand, the commercial fisherman still works harder than the average farmer and often deals with a cyclic crop that may boom one year and bust the next.

There's been a lot of romantic flap about how the Mississippi can put a spell on a man and how, once spellbound, he can never be really happy elsewhere. But a lot of rivermen would be happier almost anywhere else. The River is a harsh master whose rewards seldom equal his demands. Anyone who regards river life as a carefree slice of Americana has been spending too much time with Mark Twain, and not enough time bailing leaky jo'boats, lifting tarred web stiffened by January, or nursing hands split by exposure and wounded by poisonous catfish spines.

Commercial fishing on the Mississippi is a lean, hard, chancy way of living that demands long hours and unceasing diligence — for every hour spent ashore means nets unlifted and fish unsold. It is a hand-to-mouth existence in the truest sense, and it has defeated more men than it has sustained. The men who do succeed are, in George Kaufman's words: "too windy to drown, too mad to freeze, and too goddam ornery to call any man 'Boss'."

These are the River's own. If their work world is a rough one — and reeks of sweat, tar and bayou mud — it is nonetheless a most genuine place, peopled with genuine men.

aves

the gloomiest bird

THE CREATURE called the turkey buzzard hovers over the land like a fallen angel. A great carrion bird with a naked, raddled head and plumage like an old shroud, watching for death with his amazing eyes.

Other birds and animals do not fear him, for unlike his raptor cousins he does not bring death; he only attends it. Somewhere along the antediluvian track he specialized, losing his raptorial talons and the killing power of his feet. When the buzzard lost his ability to kill and embraced a postmortem cuisine, he became the most despised of birds.

He is certainly the ugliest. Not just homely, but repugnant in an epic, classic way. He's the Ugly Champ of America, hands down. His feathers are a rusty black edged with brown and his only color is in the naked atrocity of a head.

Yet, for all his graveyard look, he is among the most beautiful of birds on the wing. Few other American birds possess such majesty of flight. He leaves all ugliness on the earth below, and after the first wingstrokes as he labors heavily away from his carrion—and as he earns enough altitude to find the thermal updrafts and the high, tending winds — he becomes a floating mote of infinite grace.

His broad, gloomy wings may span six feet, but he is not heavy. I once picked up a dead buzzard that had been shot by a hunter. The bird was in good condition and full flesh, but weighed only five pounds. While in flight the primaries of his wing tips are spread like fingers and the head and neck are snugged in close to the body. From a distance he may appear almost headless, and unlike the eagles — with which he is often confused — his tail is never spread in flight.

Vultures are gifted with the ability to find animals in travail, and they may show interest in a creature days before it actually gives up the ghost.

Jim Keefe and I were roping a canoe up the Current River deep in the Ozarks. It's a big river down there near the Arkansas line, strong, wide and swift, and the job was made even stiffer because Keefe had three broken ribs.

Stove in as he was, Jim wheezed painfully along the gravel shingle, and a fit of coughing would double him with pain. To complete the illusion, he even smelled slightly dead. He was smoking his favorite fishing pipe, a blackened old hod with the reek of carrion.

On a bend of the Current just above the Big Barren Valley, we were joined by a large turkey vulture. It wasn't just coincidence. The bird was interested in *us*. Sometimes he swung overhead within forty yards, twisting his naked head and peering down hopefully. He escorted us for ten minutes, carefully surveying the situation and looking especially interested whenever Jim would cough or sneeze and then grimace in agony. I cheerfully pointed out the obvious connotation of this to Keefe, but he wasn't amused.

The turkey buzzard will eat anything that's dead, finding his carrion from immense heights by sight, not scent. Cover a carcass with grass or weeds and the vulture will never find it. Someone once stuffed a deerskin with grass and a vulture ripped it to shreds before he realized he'd been bilked. In fact, the vultures' sense of smell may even be deficient. If it weren't he couldn't live with himself. A turkey buzzard has an air about him, and in my experience he is easily the raunchiest, ripest creature that breathes. Part of this is caused by certain natural oils in his plumage, and part by his feeding and nesting habits. Whatever it is, I only know that a buzzard stinks to high heaven and no one but a case-hardened biologist can stand to investigate him closely.

Some years ago, a friend of mine moved in with a family of buzzards in an Ozark cave to escape a violent summer thunderstorm. In short order he became a vulture expert.

When a buzzard is gorged with carrion, he may be too heavy for a quick takeoff in an emergency. So he just salvoes his payload by regurgitating until he's light enough to fly. This nervous response to danger is also a defense, and both young and old buzzards can vomit accurately and forcefully when frightened. That's what my friend learned in that Ozark cave, although it was a couple of years before he could bear to speak of it and he never did manage to be objective about the affair.

Repugnant as the vultures seem to us, they are superbly adapted to their way of life. They have some of the most splendid eyes in nature. A vulture can mark a dead rabbit in a field when the bird is nearly out of sight in a blank sky. The great wings are constructed for tireless soaring, and the beak is designed for tearing flesh, with outer nostrils passing entirely through the beak and the inner nostrils opening from within the beak. This prevents clogging of the nostrils by food, and the featherless head is easily kept clean when plunged into the depths of a putrescent carcass.

The vulturine digestive tract must be sheathed with tool steel, for it can withstand powerful toxins that are lethal to most other warm-blooded creatures.

One of the most potent natural poisons known is the

metabolic by-product of the bacterium *Clostridium botulinus*. The toxin of one of this bacterium's types is responsible for the sweeping botulism plagues that kill hundreds of thousands of ducks at a whack. The chemicals produced by this tiny germ cause a form of violent food poisoning — a sort of super ptomaine. Yet, the turkey vulture can resist a dose of *botulinus* toxin that will kill 300,000 guinea pigs.

So if it's dead, the turkey vulture can safely eat it. The big birds are a prized sanitation corps down south, for a flock of the birds can reduce a dead cow to shining bones in a few days. A southern farmer seldom needs to bury dead stock, but just drags it to some remote corner of his place and forgets about it. The vultures take over from there.

In old Charleston, black and turkey buzzards once roamed the streets like sparrows, cleaning up any refuse that was edible. There, as in most parts of the country, it was not only against the law to kill vultures but also against public opinion, and I've yet to see any part of the country that doesn't take a mighty dim view of vulture-shooters. The big birds harm neither domestic stock, wildlife, nor man's interests. At one time there was a flurry of concern when the turkey buzzard was accused of being a vector of hog cholera, but Florida researchers acquitted him. Even the virus of hog cholera apparently can't survive the vulture's digestive tract, and the disease is not transmissible through the bird.

Primitive man still regards the vulture as a messmate, although modern man reviles the bird because of its table manners and diet. This is only one of the affectations we've developed since we've moved out of the woods and uptown, for it hasn't been long since our kinfolks dined together with vultures from the same ripening carcasses.

We're older now, and infinitely more polished. We know what's good for us and we eat our fresh meat and vegetables and try desperately to live for eighty years. But the buzzard still clings to his foul carrion fare, gives us a sepulchral horselaugh, and lives to be 118!

the grand passage

AN OLD GANDER raised his head from a meal of three-square grass and stretched his wings in the warm Louisiana sun. Nearby, other blue geese were launching themselves into the air, and the gander rose to join them. For nearly an hour they wheeled together over the wet pastures of *paille des oies* before they settled down again to resume feeding.

For a week a restlessness had been growing among them and they rose more often on short flights. It was nearly the last of February. Songbirds were building nests and the days were becoming longer and hotter. Still the geese remained, as if they knew that their distant summering grounds were locked by winter and that spring blizzards still raged on Baffin Island.

Then, one day in early March, the blue gander rose from the marshes of the Sabine Refuge and joined a large band of geese near the Bayou Constance. Two other huge Louisiana flocks also were forming, one above the flats east of the Mississippi's mouth and another near the *Chenier du Tigre*.

These three great flocks, with an honor guard of snow geese, rose a thousand feet above the Louisiana tidal marshes and swung into the north — to be joined by more flocks of sparkling snow geese coming up from the wintering grounds on the gulf coast of Texas and western Louisiana. In a steady, direct course up the face of a continent and up the great chute of the Mississippi Valley the birds flew, overtaking early pintails, mallards and a few Canada geese.

Through western Arkansas they flew, and over western Missouri where they found and followed the coffee-colored bends of the Missouri River. And now their momentum was checked for they struck the barrier of the thirty-degree isotherm. They had left Louisiana in summer, had flown through spring, and as they reached southwestern Iowa they caught up with the last of winter.

They rested there, the countless geese piling up on the threshold of winter. Around Forney's Lake, Kellogg Slough, the Green Bottoms and Lake Manawa south of Council Bluffs there were single flocks of a hundred thousand blue and snow geese. In fields near Percival and McPaul there were geese almost beyond number by the seventeenth of March, feeding on shattered corn left last autumn by the cornpickers, and on the gumbo fields washed with the first greens of winter wheat. Men tried futilely to estimate their number and gave up, shaking their heads in wonder at eighty-acre fields solid with birds.

I walked out on a sandspit of the Plum Creek Washout late one night, and the sounds of the geese settling down to sleep were like standing on the shore of an ocean. I clapped my hands, commanding silence for a brief, blank instant, and then a clap of thunder replied. A vast wall of geese eclipsed the moon and sky. First there was the windy roar of a quarter-million wings and then the bedlam din of barking geese flying in the night.

In river towns, street lights attracting newly-arrived flocks were turned off to end the ceaseless clamor of circling geese and give the townsmen some sleep. Nearly every snow and blue goose in the New World was crammed into a strip of Missouri River valley sixty miles long and twenty miles wide.

But by late March the last barriers of midwestern winter were collapsing, and by the first of April the geese were nearly gone from Iowa and Nebraska.

Northward, through April, the Dakotas and Manitoba. For nearly a week the great, broken lines stitched the sky over Winnipeg and vanished into the northeast. Then, for seven hundred miles, no more was known of them. No man saw them again until a Cree trapper north of James Bay looked up late one May morning and made out a skein of blue geese flying over the pack ice of Hudson's Bay, making for the reeking mud flats and barren tundra of Baffin and Southampton Islands.

The blue geese nested there in the chilling rains of mid-June, a little more than three months since their departure from the Bayou Constance nearly three thousand miles to the south. The greater mass of snow geese split off and went "beyond the north wind" — the place that named them — to the arctic coast of Canada within fifteen degrees of the North Pole. Like the blues, they nested in an empty land more water than earth.

Perhaps the birds follow routes dictated to them by ancient ice caps. Maybe the ice sheets of the glacial ages drove all life before them and birds moved north or south as the glaciers receded or advanced, and perhaps these great racial movements became habits that are unbroken today.

Or maybe the north was the old ancestral home of all birds and was once a fair, warm land in which they could live all year. Perhaps that is why birds, still dreaming of a distant past, seek the old home ranges each spring. Or the ancestral home could have been in the south, but so many birds concentrated there that it became impossible for all to feed, and so some began flying north in the spring to lands where there was less competition.

Certainly, geese move north in the spring as advancing seasons unlock food supplies in the subarctic. In turn, they

A rare and unusual photo of a lone blue goose flying 3,000 feet above the flat western Iowa landscape.

are forced south when winter threatens to cut off these rations. A few men have reflected that birds go north to avoid the many enemies of the southland and seek safety for their nests in the Land of Little Sticks.

It's also known that geese respond to waxing and waning light, and that their gonads increase in size and function as light periods grow longer. There's a theory of "photoperiodism" that holds that total light quantity influences the state of the sex organs, causing northern migration with increasing day length in the spring, and southern migration as northern daylight wanes in autumn.

But all these are only conjectures and no man will probably ever know the truth.

And many men, although they wonder at the grand passage, do not really care for a solution. They only know that the geese keep a tryst in the north when winter has ended, and knowing that is enough.

man and the mallard

LIKE ALL LIVING things, the mallard duck is the fruit of its environment. As that environment frowns or smiles, the mallard fails or flourishes.

Modern man is also a product of environment, but unlike the mallard he is not content to simply exist within it. He must dominate it. As man frowns or smiles, all environments — including the mallard's — fail or flourish.

The first mallard environment to be invaded by modern man was the flyway systems that link the northern breeding areas with the wintering grounds. But mallards are opportunists that are quick to see advantage in a new situation. As man has captured the waterfowl flyways the mallard has adapted itself to cornfields, reservoirs, farm ponds, and even popcorn handouts from kids in city parks.

The ancient flyway routes became great pantries of corn, oats, soybeans, rice and wheat that are heavily used by migrant and resident mallards. Much of this is waste; it's been estimated that ten percent of the midwestern corn crop may be left in the fields, and the canny mallard is quick to find it. However, mallards can also cause serious depredation of unharvested crops where man has usurped their natural feeding grounds. Hardy and resistant to cold, often lingering in the north long after other ducks have headed south, they may ravage croplands day or night.

In Colorado, where 1½ million mallards congregated in January on the Arkansas and Platte River drainages, it was estimated that the huge flocks had a daily capacity of $4,500 worth of corn. The annual California rice loss to ducks may amount to a million dollars, with $750,000 more lost in other cereal grains, alfalfa and lettuce. Most of this damage is due to pintails, but mallards get their share. Special hunting seasons have been set in an effort to curb mallard crop damage, and Arkansas schoolboys used to take shotguns to school and be picked up in late afternoon by farm trucks that drove them to the rice fields for the daily bout with flocks of hungry mallards.

The most serious mallard damage is in the southern Canadian prairie provinces where clouds of mallards raid wheat fields. This is nothing new, but it has become more serious since 1945. High post-war grain prices caused farming to expand into mallard nesting grounds where large concentrations of ducks quickly acquired a taste for corn and wheat.

To make matters worse, many Canadian farmers now swath wheat before it is combined, rather than cutting it with binders and shocking it. This swathed wheat, strewn over miles of prairie, is a picnic for ducks. Some Canadian farm losses have run as high as eighty percent. In three municipalities in Saskatchewan — averaging eleven townships in size — annual mallard damage has amounted to nearly $275,000. To farmers who may lose an average of one wheat crop in seven to mallards, ducks become implacable enemies.

Just as the mallard is swift to exploit man-made fields

that have replaced his natural feeding grounds, he is quick to find man-made water areas that appear along the flyways. Mallards use countless stock ponds and farm ponds that did not exist a few years ago. In South Dakota, artificial stock ponds may produce at least 200,000 ducks a year, and irrigated lands on the west coast offer grassy-banked ditches to nesting mallards.

An immense mallard-holding force is exerted by the chain of reservoirs up the Missouri River. Mallards stay on these huge impoundments all winter if nearby feeder fields are clear of ice and snow, and large segments of the southbound flights are halted by such areas as Fort Randall, Gavin's Point, Fort Peck, Lake Andes and others. On December 22, 1958, over a million ducks were counted on the Fort Randall reservoir and it was estimated that year that 1,300,000 ducks wintered in South Dakota. From 1955 to 1958, a December average of 831,000 ducks was found on the Fort Randall impoundment alone.

New lakes, ponds and reservoirs — and a hardbitten disregard for winter — keep many mallards in the north. Nearly three million of them were censused during January, 1956, in Minnesota, Wisconsin, Ohio, Indiana, Illinois, Iowa and Missouri; and within this region there were more mallards wintering north of the Ohio River than south of it.

No other duck is so rugged a pioneer, nor so capable of meeting emergencies. In spring, 1959, when vast stretches of the southern Canadian nesting grounds were stricken by drought and thousands of potholes were blowing dust, the arriving mallards simply kept going. While such species as the canvasback waited hopelessly on dwindling marshes, the mallards pressed on to northern Alberta and Saskatchewan, the Yukon and Northwest Territories — forbidding tundra regions where nesting conditions were very poor for ducks but where there is always water. Although the drought was a crippling blow to the mallard population, it was disastrous to stay-at-home canvasbacks and redheads.

A year later many of the Canadian potholes were again filled with water and the mallards returned to their traditional nesting grounds. In 1959, over 270,000 mallards were counted in one area of the Northwest Territories. The same region in 1960 held only 47,500 mallards. When drought demanded it, the mallards had pioneered north to survive; when the situation in the south improved, they had come home.

This shrewd adaptiveness is most apparent whenever man and the mallard match wits.

Duck clubs near Havana, Illinois, used to end their shooting at noon during the days when baiting of ducks was lawful. With all shooting ended at noon, the mallards soon began returning to the strewn corn about a half-hour later. So the club operators extended shooting until 1:00 p.m. The mallards quickly tumbled to this change and stayed away from the baited areas until 1:30. When shooting was extended to 2 p.m., the mallards didn't return until nearly 3 p.m. And so it went — the shooting hours being set later and the mallards adjusting their own schedule accordingly. By the end of the season, shooting extended to dark and the ducks were feeding at night; as fast as man adapted himself to the situation, the mallards followed suit.

Smart as they are before, mallards graduate from college once they've been stung by a few shot pellets. Banded mallards that are known to have been wounded show a much lower band recovery than unwounded birds, indicating a learned wariness. Many other game birds also grow wary when the gun pressure is turned on. But unlike most of these, mallards may be inflexibly wild while being heavily hunted, or may live with man in perfect harmony and grow fat and tame on barnyard ponds.

Although the mallard can salvage many benefits from man's domination of the flyways, it cannot withstand human destruction of the northern breeding grounds. There has been more mallard breeding habitat destroyed in the past fifty years than in all the previous history of our continent.

The finest mallard breeding grounds in the United States are the prairies of the upper midwest. This is the southern fringe of the great continental duck factory and only a few years ago it produced up to five million ducks each year. But it also lies in the farm belt, and by 1953 it was estimated that agricultural drainage had destroyed from one-half to two-thirds of the pothole country's duck-producing capacity.

Iowa once had nearly three million acres of marsh and potholes, and probably twice that in wet years. But those primeval duck nurseries are long gone, drained down bull ditches that were cut by huge plows and lines of oxen, then through smaller channels cut by ditching spades, and today's final trickles are vanishing down tile lines into straightened rivers.

Half of Minnesota's original ten million acres of wetlands has been destroyed. Over three million acres were lost during the 21 years from 1937 to 1958 alone. In one township of west-central Minnesota, sixteen percent of the water areas were drained in only five years.

In North Dakota, intensive drainage began in the early 1940's and shifted into high gear during the "Fatal Fifties." From 1943 to 1958, North Dakota lost about 135,000 water areas, including 20,000 potholes in some of the finest duck breeding grounds in North America.

In one thirty-seven-county area in South Dakota, 48,147 acres of wetlands vanished between 1951 and 1959. About one-fourth of South Dakota's potholes have been emptied since 1944.

Much of this drainage has been paid for by the very duck hunters who abhor it.

Since 1943, well over a million acres of wetlands have been drained in the upper midwest with the aid of federal funds. Under a federal drainage program, a farmer can apply for aid and be paid on the basis of the number of cubic yards of earth removed from ditches. This subsidy runs as high as fifty percent — a strong incentive for a farmer to drain a marsh or pothole on his land. In addition, the government provides all the valuable and necessary engineering and planning free of charge.

Of the 1,350,000 prairie potholes in the upper Midwest, more than 350,000 have been eliminated through federal subsidy payments. From 1940 to 1953, almost 1,700,000 acres of wetlands were destroyed with the aid of taxpayers' money.

In a brilliant game of bureaucratic pingpong, federal agencies subsidized much of this drainage at the same time the U.S. Fish and Wildlife Service sought to acquire and develop more public wetlands and waterfowl areas. Competing with the massive federal drainage programs has been a hopeless contest. In 1955 it was estimated that if the Fish and Wildlife Service were to maintain current waterfowl production in the pothole country by buying the 63,000 acres of potholes that were then being lost annually, it would cost at least ten million dollars. From 1951 to 1955, eighty-three times as much money was spent by the government to destroy 256,000 acres of waterfowl habitat as the Fish and Wildlife Service spent from duck stamp funds to save only 3,462 acres of wetlands in the same three states!

Most of this man-made drought has been to increase crop production. In other words, a federal agency helps foot the bill to drain more land to raise more crops to add to the nation's farm surplus woes, and with the other hand pays farmers to build ponds and retire croplands under the conservation and acreage reserve phases of the soil bank program. At the same time, the federal agency charged with waterfowl conservation is striving manfully to salvage some of the native wetlands that its sister services pay landowners to drain.

This federal drainage program is clad in the commendable garb of "conservation." However, it is difficult to understand how that term can be applied to practices that promote soil erosion by speeding water runoff, add to flood crests, and wreak injury to the land and wildlife in an effort to boost production of crops that not only aren't needed but which may not even be the most suitable crops for the particular soil type!

But this cloudbank of confusion shows some promise of clearing. In summer, 1960, a "Farm Drainage Treaty" was drawn up between the departments of Interior and Agriculture. Affecting the 89-county pothole region of western Minnesota and the Dakotas, the agreement provides that county ASC committees notify the Fish and Wildlife Service before approving any drainage assistance. Federal waterfowl experts will then investigate that particular area and report any objections to the ASC committee. Such inspection also gives the Service a chance to buy wetlands suitable for waterfowl.

* * * *

Man has struck a body blow at flyway environment, but the wild mallard has managed to roll with punches that have some other duck species groggy and reeling. However, the mallard cannot tolerate abuse of its breeding habitat nor survive a production collapse in drained, barren pothole country. Even though the bulk of our mallards is produced in Canada's prairie provinces, this does not justify squandering the breeding grounds that still survive in the United States.

It's painful to know that our waterfowl resource is threadbare and that the great abundances faded so quickly, so easily. Painful, too, is the knowledge that we are no longer young hunters in a young land. We have spent our youth and much of our natural wealth in a headlong rush of technology. We are children prematurely gray, still looking wistfully backward and reluctant to admit that our boyhood heroes — the Fred Kimbles and the Captain Bogarduses — have passed, and with them the immeasurable flights of wildfowl.

But in place of youth and its openhanded waste there are the first signs of maturity and a growing caution. A new wind is rising, fanning the embers of old campfires, and we are slowly beginning to shape a national conservation conscience.

The depth of that conscience will spell the fates of resources more valuable than ducks. But to what end, if the marshes are emptied and our mallards fly away while we sleep?

the bird machine

A BIRD IS A flash of color, a burst of song, or a high, aloof vigilance. It can be all gentleness and soft appeal, or baleful, raptorial harshness. It may be loathesome or lovable; regal or revolting. But stripped of all man-given personality, the bird is a fantastic mechanism hung with an array of Rube Goldberg gadgets that make life more liveable.

The basic bird is a rigid framework from which all needless weight has been jettisoned. The bony basket of its skeleton has become fused, discarding excess linkages, muscles and ligaments. Unlike the mammals, reptiles and fish, birds do not need flexible bodies. Their needs are served by moveable necks, legs and wings.

Those wings, with their spars of light, hollow bone, are powered by an air-cooled engine of great economy. A bird's rather small, compact lungs are connected to big air sacs throughout its body. One of these sacs even leads out into the hollow wing bones. It is possible that a bird's high internal heat is dissipated into these air sacs and then passed

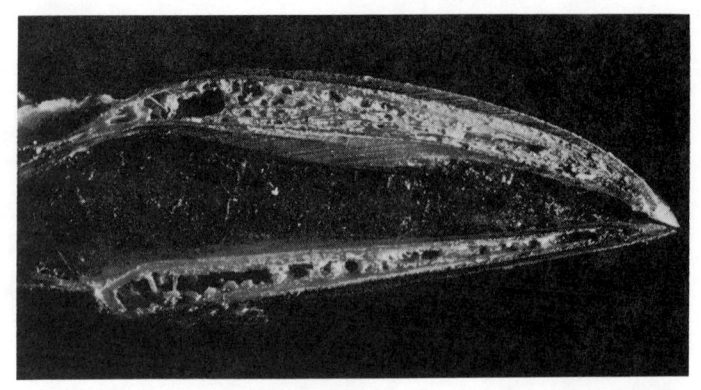

A cross-section of blackbird's bill shows the peculiar sharp ridge in the palate, which serves to slice through acorns and other thin-shelled fruits.

out through the lungs, and the sacs may even complement the lungs in gas exchange and breathing. By comparison, man's engine is liquid-cooled and the sort of clumsy design you'd expect in a groundling.

As a further adaptation for flight, birds have traded heavy jaws and teeth for light, horny beaks. Some birds — the plant and seed eaters — have developed gizzards. This is not a concession to lightness alone, for a bird's heavy gizzard may weigh more than the jaws and teeth it replaces. But a gizzard puts the chewing mechanism back near the center of gravity where weight belongs in a flying machine.

The gizzard itself is a remarkable tool. A mallard duck's gizzard can easily crush hickory nuts, and the gizzard of a Canada goose is lined with stony plates that grind food like millstones. Like our skins, the inner lining of a bird's gizzard is being constantly sloughed off and replaced; in such birds as doves and pigeons it breaks up to form "pigeon milk" that is regurgitated for the nestlings.

The gadgets of bird structure include a wild array of tongues, beaks and eyes. Tongues with brushes, rasps, tubes and barbed spears. Beaks with hooks, shovels, probes, chisels, flexible tips and sieves. One of the strangest beaks is that of the common grackle, the blackbird that swaggers brassily around your front lawn. In the palate of the upper bill is a knifelike ridge. The grackle can pick up an acorn, rotate it in its beak, and neatly cut through the shell which falls away in two halves.

The most famous beak is the pelican's, with its huge gular pouch for shipping fish. But this isn't unique to the pelicans; certain thrushes high in alpine regions where the insect hunting is poor have deep throat pouches opening into the rear of the mouth. The bird fills these pouches with food on an extended hunt, and eats at leisure.

Then there are the eyes — the magnificent, all-seeing eyes of birds. Few mammals can match them, and the eyes of some hawks are eight times as powerful as man's. A duck hawk, for instance, can sight prey at incredible distances and may begin his screaming "stoop" on a flock of teal long before a watching man can see him. To do this, the duck hawk must not only have eyes of great acuity but also of great accommodation — the ability to change the shape of the eye and constantly refocus. To miscalculate would mean death, for a duck hawk's terminal velocity may be nearly 200 miles per hour, and I have seen such stooping falcons

A woodpecker's skull shows the long, strong, chisel-like bill necessary for tearing away wood. A cartilaginous pad at the base of this bill serves to cushion the incessant hammering shock that would otherwise be transmitted to the brain. The base of the woodpecker's tongue actually extends back into the skull, greatly lengthening the organ that must probe into wood cavities for insects.

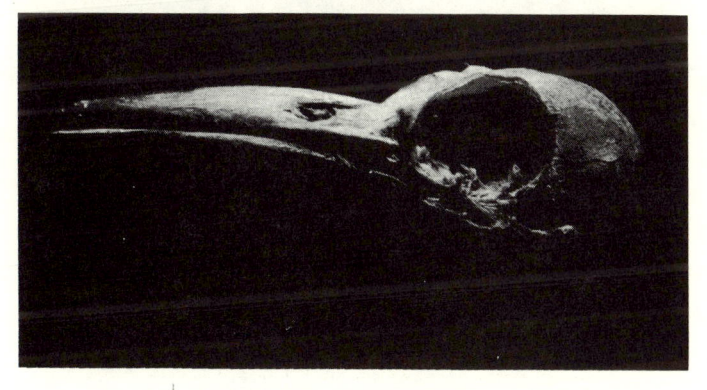

A hunting short-eared owl clearly shows the peculiar facial disk of the species. Some scientists think this odd "face" tends to catch and focus light into the eye area, increasing vision at dusk or night.

Since the eyes of owls are fixed in the sockets and are immovable, it is thought that owls must rotate their heads to scan their surroundings. This head rotation may be as much as 180°, as demonstrated in this picture of a short-eared owl apparently looking directly behind itself.

recover from their dives a scant thirty feet above the ground.
Just as remarkable are the eyes of the night shift — the owls. These huge yellow and black orbs are infinitely sensitive. They may be a hundred times more receptive in low light intensity than man's. Some owls can hunt — with difficulty — in light ranging down to the equivalent of the amount shed by an ordinary candle at nearly half a mile!

But other creatures have wings, keen eyes and light bones. One thing, however, sets birds completely apart from all other life forms; nothing else in the world has feathers.

These are highly modified scales, legacies from the birds' reptilian ancestors. Flat, strong and stiff, without brittleness nor weight, they shingle a bird's body with warmth and form a remarkable airfoil.

The young feather begins as a hollow cylinder with a tightly-rolled vane fitted within. At this state it is a pinfeather, set in a pocket of skin with its hollow base fitted over a small "papilla" or knob. As the feather grows, its hollow quill takes blood and nourishment from the papilla. At feather maturity, the blood supply is cut off and the feather becomes a dead, stiff substance without sensation. The papilla becomes dormant although it still fits into the base of the feather. If the feather is removed, the papilla is stimulated and a new feather begins to form immediately.

The hollow, basal end of the feather is the quill. At about the place where the webbing of the feather begins, this quill becomes solid and flexible and is called the "shaft" or *rachis*. From this shaft grows the web, or vane, of the feather — a masterwork of design and function.

Extending from the main feather shaft are barbs, the main branches of the feather webbing. From these barbs branch the little barbules, fibers armed with tiny hooks. These infinitesimal crochet hooks, called "barbicels," interlock tightly with those of adjacent barbs to form the dense, stiff webbing that is the flight plane of the avian wing.

The highest degree of this interlocking is in the stiff, strong flight feathers of the tail and wings. Without it, the feathers would be soft and fluffy. If the shaft is lengthened and the barbules and barbicels are completely lacking, there is a delicate plume.

Clothing the bird densely and giving the body its soft, rounded shape are the contour feathers. These smaller feathers are not as densely webbed as the stiff primaries of the wings, and are much softer. Beneath them are the *plumulae,* the down feathers of exquisite softness. These fluffy feather tufts lack a central shaft and the barbs branch directly from the hollow quill. With almost no weight or bulk, down feathers are a near-perfect insulation material that even man, with all his miracle fibers, has never been able to improve on.

Some herons have a strange "powder down." Bitterns, for example, have no oil glands in their skins for cleansing and lubrication. They rely on a fine powder produced by the automatic pulverization of some down feathers. This material is of talcum fineness and soothes the bird's skin and helps lubricate and waterproof the plumage. In such birds as the black-crowned night heron it is even slightly luminous.

Sometime in late summer — usually in August — most of our songbirds moult. The worn, year-old feathers are discarded and new flight equipment grows in. Moulting always begins in a certain area of the bird's body and proceeds in a very orderly way. Only when the growth of the new feather is well underway is the next feather discarded. By the time a third or fourth feather is shed, the first one is nearly full-grown.

Most birds do not lose flight and mobility while losing plumage. No old feathers are shed until adjacent new feathers take their places. In their "eclipse" moult, ducks lose their flight powers while moulting but are able to swim to safety and do not need flight for feeding or survival. For a brief period, they can afford to lose their wings. This

The feather barbs of an owl lack the tight, close interlocking of the tiny hooked barbules, resulting in soft feathers that are virtually soundless in flight. The owl's generally fluffy plumage — like that of the whippoorwills and nighthawks — indicate a bird not so highly evolved as hard-feathered species.

This magnified photograph of the feather barbs of an eagle show the dense, close interlocking of the barbules that results in stiff, "hard" feathers. Such feathers are characteristic of most of the "higher" birds.

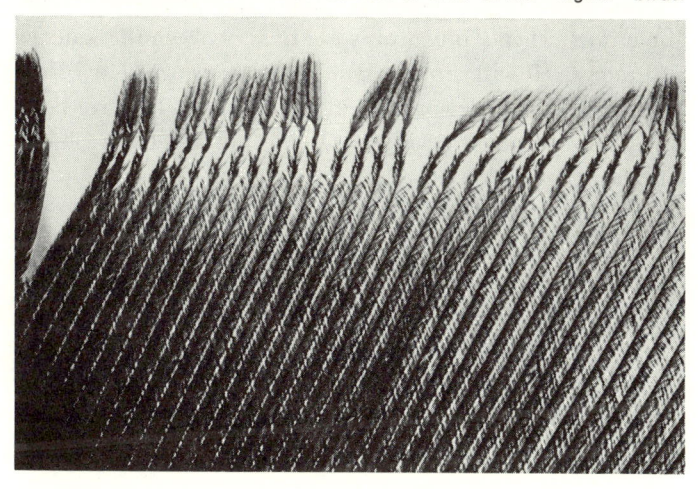

eclipse moult, which is unique in waterfowl, occurs only in the northern hemisphere. It does not take place south of the equator, even among species of ducks that inhabit both hemispheres.

During the moult, many birds become shy and cease any singing or bold display as if they realize they aren't quite their old selves. Or perhaps, as some old stories have it, they are grieving over their lost beauty. If they are, they are fooling themselves as much as they fool us, for the great beauty of many birds is illusion.

Only three true color pigments exist in most feathers: reds, yellows and browns. All other colors are apparent, caused by the refraction of light. Although a few tropical birds do have green color pigment, most greens are caused by yellow or brown pigment overlaid with a thin material that refracts light and gives the impression of green. A drake mallard's head is not green; it is nearly black. The green is caused by much the same phenomenon as an oil "rainbow" on water. Like most blues, violets and metallic colors in birds, the mallard's green head is caused by a shattering of the light spectrum.

Nor is an indigo bunting indigo, nor a bluebird blue. Sometimes, when a bluebird is wet or is between the watcher and the sun, it will show its true colors — brownish or black.

An odd and noteworthy thing, maybe, but I'd have been just as happy not knowing it. I like my bluebirds blue — true blue.

child of adversity

THERE WAS THIS dude duck hunter at Big Wall Lake who'd just come ashore and was loading his new hunting gear into his new car. Warren Wilson was working the marsh that day, and walked up to check the man's license and see how he'd made out.

"Got three ducks," the hunter said.

"Fine," said Warren. "Mind if I see them?"

The hunter opened his car trunk and grandly indicated three defunct mudhens.

"Say," said Warren, "those are all right! What kind of ducks do you call those?"

"Oh, just average run," the hunter replied with proud vagueness.

Which is the story of the mudhen's life — average run. There's not a whole lot you can say about him; most duck hunters know him but only the dudes pay much attention to him. He just isn't the kind of critter that fires your imagination.

He looks something like a chicken-faced duck, a dark, muddy bird with a white, henlike bill and green feet that are out of all proportion to the rest of him. Big feet they are, with long toes that are lobed and not webbed like a duck's. For whatever it's worth, the mudhen, or coot, isn't a duck, but a shorebird that's taken up swimming.

As he swims, his neck and head pump in unison with the strokes of his long green legs. He doesn't erupt from the marsh's surface like a puddle duck, but sort of trots along the water until he gets up flying speed, leaving a long trail of splashes in his wake. When he's tearing along at about ten miles per hour — and if a hunter doesn't cut him down — he rises into the air in low, heavy flight.

Coots may be all over the place during duck season. Novice hunters may shoot them for "black mallards," and veteran hunters may pop one occasionally for practice or ignore them completely. Mudhens never really seem to grow gun-wise, but gallop from one duck blind to another in an aimless sort of way as if pleading with hunters to do them the honor of mistaking them for mallards or something.

There are a few hunters who say they like to eat mudhens and, when the birds have been feeding on something like wild celery, they aren't half-bad. None of the mudhens I have eaten were as skunky as some bluebills can be. When it comes to that, there are even mallards and canvasbacks that can drive a cook out of a kitchen. But there's one thing about a coot; if you like gizzards he's your dish, because a coot's innards are mostly gizzard.

It is strange how local tradition can dictate contempt for certain creatures. In Europe, the carp is a highly-prized food fish and in many eastern states the groundhog is a protected game animal. It's the same with the mudhen. In some places the bird is called a "whitebill" or a "rice hen" and is a welcome part of the bag. Like on the Fox Lakes in northern Illinois — where opening day sounds like a Juarez election — and where the mudhen is a very big thing and

Chicago hunters will fistfight over a skinny coot that's been shot to dollrags. It's a matter of relative abundance, rather than basic quality. The severest indictments against the mudhen are its availability and bumbling conduct. A coot is just about as smart as a redhead, and if he was as rare he'd probably be just as prized.

Some old hunters welcome coots on a marsh, for they add life to a spread of decoys and make them more effective. Mudhens detract nothing from a marsh and, if anything, help impart a sense of humor to an otherwise humorless wetland.

Yet, some hunters delight in scragging mudhens — usually out of sheer boredom, bloodlust, or as proof of their shooting ability. Boredom and bloodlust are valid motives, if not defensible, but it's hard to savvy the hunter who shoots mudhens "for the fun of it" for this is about as much fun as shotgunning a hat hung in a tree.

That's a favorite personal gripe of mine, for few things wrench me more than seeing a small, dowdy cluster of crippled mudhens awaiting death around the last open water of a freezing marsh. They have no nobility in their dying; they are stricken buffoons, homely and ungraceful to the end, waiting for foxes, minks or January to find them.

If anything, I feel even more sympathy for those mudhens than I do for mallards in the same situation, for the coots were shot in idleness and a sort of off-handed contempt, and not from any desire of possession. They were simply shot for the shooting and, unlike the regal mallard that droops beside them, they pass unwanted and unmourned.

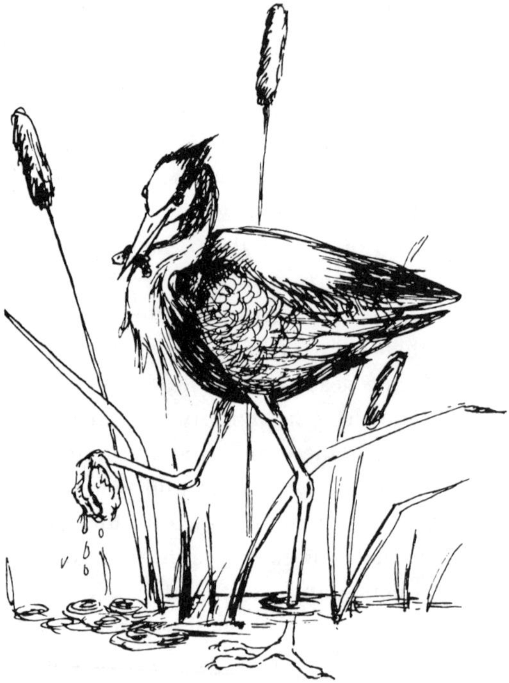

heron summer

THE ROOKERY WAS somewhere just ahead in the dense tongue of lowland forest between the Nishnabotna and Missouri rivers.

By noon we could see that the herons owned the best part of this forest — the airy upper part. Rusty Morgan and I were in the dense, fetid understory and before we had walked a half-mile our shirts were plastered to our backs and black with mosquitoes.

It was a flood plain jungle of huge sycamores, soft maples and cottonwoods whose canopies locked together far above us to shut out most of the sun. Vines of poison ivy as thick as a man's wrist grew up some of the trees. The soft gumbo pan on which we walked was a tangle of bedstraw, stinging nettle, horseweeds, and dense beds of poison ivy in its ground form. Over it all, now that the late May floodwaters had receded, there was a singing veil of mosquitoes and dog-belly gnats.

Rusty finally stopped and waved me up to him.

"They're up there just ahead," he said. "It ain't so bad in here, now. But you ought to hear it at night. You'd swear you was in the middle of the Congo or someplace."

In the upper stories of the big trees ahead there was a muted clattering like a flock of blackbirds in a distant marsh. Rusty and I put out our cigarettes and tried to move on more slowly and quietly, but we didn't make it. The clattering stopped, and after a hanging moment of silence there was a bedlam of harsh clucks, whoops and rusty creaks. Then there were blue herons in the air above us, scolding and swearing, their six-foot wings noiseless above the trees.

The foliage was a bit thinner here, and in the tops of the trees all around us — never less than forty feet above the ground — we could see the huge nests. Some were nearly four feet in diameter, great stick structures that were visible for miles when the trees were leafless. I had seen the rookery two years before from the other side of the valley during the March goose flight. It was one of the largest on the Missouri River, nearly twenty acres of heron nests in an isolated river forest that was seldom visited by man during the nesting season.

In a sense, I had dreaded this visit. I was leery of walking under the great rookery, having an awe of herons that's akin to my respect for skunks, buzzards and carsick puppies.

For nothing on earth can equal the cosmic, monumental defecation of a startled heron. Several times, while canoeing close-in to riverbanks, I have been almost beneath perching herons before they saw me. As the startled birds lumbered into the air they voided incredible ropes of excrement that could have whitewashed an entire fleet of canoes. One startled heron is bad enough; a whole heronry could be a catastrophe.

However, you don't startle herons when you sneak into

their rookery. They'll know you're coming; you aren't fooling anyone. By the time we entered the heronry and moved in under the nest sycamores, the colony of herons was wheeling and yelling above the high trees but, praise be, there wasn't an unpuckered sphincter in the entire grove.

Rusty moved over to a patch of sunlight that filtered down through the treetops, and sat down on a punky log where he could watch the crown of a huge sycamore. I joined him there, where the sunlight helped with the gnats and mosquitoes. We sat and watched the four nests in the top of the tree. There were still herons circling over the rookery, making their rusty-gate noises, but they were beginning to settle down.

Scattered on the ground beneath the trees were some large fragments of bluish-green eggshells. I picked up one of the egg caps and saw the even serration of its broken edge. Somewhere in the green canopy sixty feet above us, heron nestlings had pipped their eggshells only a few days before.

Normally, blue herons play a lone hand, colonizing only during the breeding season and avoiding man whenever possible. But now the young were hatching and the old herons were bolder. Their rookery was "ripe" and they had abandoned much of their normal caution, just as their snowy egret cousins once did in the Florida rookeries when they circled and called helplessly over their nests as plume hunters shot them down for the filmy aigrettes of their nuptial plumage.

Rusty and I stayed doggo, trying to ignore the mosquitoes, and soon the herons were landing again in their colony trees, their cheeks and necks fluttering with indignation. They were imposing birds, slaty blue above and black beneath, standing four feet tall and with wings spanning two yards. They floated easily into the high perches, settling as lightly as plumes of smoke into the thin foliage of the sycamores. But for all their size, the huge birds are mostly bones and underwear and will seldom weigh much over seven pounds.

As a boy, I once stalked and shot a great blue heron. In what was probably my only flush of academic fervor that summer, I carefully plucked the big bird there on the riverbank to examine it. I'd always wondered why herons were so hard to hit with a rifle; that day I found out. Although great blue herons stand nearly as tall as a boy, they are little more than co-ordinated sets of long legs, beaks, necks, huge wings and spearlike beaks. The plucked body of my heron didn't seem much larger than a big, skinny rooster's, and it was pathetically grotesque without the slaty plumage.

But there above us, not thirty yards away, the herons were something to see. We could watch the treetops pretty well from where we were and from the lack of small activity above — and the presence of fresh eggshells on the ground — we figured that the young birds had hatched very recently. In a few more weeks they would leave the nests and clamber among the tree limbs, sometimes even falling to the ground.

Once on the ground, a young blue heron can be easily caught by a man. But catching any great blue heron, flightless or not, young or old, isn't very smart. With its neck curved in a powerful S, a great blue heron can strike as swiftly as a snake and drive its beak completely through the blade of a pine boat oar. Striking with uncanny accuracy, it often tries for a man's eyes. A friend of ours was taking a blue heron from an exhibit cage when he was struck by the angry bird. The blow was aimed directly at his eyes but was deflected by his glasses, inflicting an ugly gash in his forehead.

With this six-inch beak, the great blue heron is a master fisher and hunter. I have lain on riverbanks for hours, watching herons wade slowly in the shoals off sandbars and sometimes standing motionless for twenty minutes at a time before flashing that deadly dart. One great blue heron in an Oklahoma river, while spearing a fish between its feet, tripped itself up. The bird floated downstream on its back with its long legs sticking into the air, trying to regain its equilibrium and dignity. But it caught the fish!

Herons don't miss their fish very often, although they may wound more than they kill, and they can raise hob in the shallow holding ponds of a fish hatchery for they are capable of taking fish that weigh well over a pound. They'll hunt other things, too. Several times, on pasture hills beside marshes, I have seen blue herons slowly stalking along grassy hillsides hunting for insects, and possibly for meadow mice or even ground squirrels.

As Rusty and I hunkered there under the sycamores and the commotion above us died down to the routine grackle-clatter of peaceful herons, birds began drifting back to their nests. Some were returning from the backwaters of the nearby Missouri with their crops distended with half-digested fish that they would regurgitate into the maws of their nestlings. The approach and landing seldom varied. A heron would circle the rookery warily and then approach her nest, floating in over the treetops on immense pinions. As she approached the crown of the tree she would slowly back-pedal her great wings to kill all flying speed and drop lightly in on the landing limb in her last airborne instant. Then she would fold up her wings in several neat gestures, look furtively around her in the manner of a grand lady finding that her slip is showing, and side-step primly along the limb to her nest.

All of this was most noteworthy, but it lost some of its flavor when viewed through a curtain of mosquitoes. We took it for a couple of more hours until our cigarettes ran out and our smudge failed. Then we stood up and moved on, and the herons began their circling and creaking and cheek-fluttering all over again.

Some of them were still at it when we topped the levee forty minutes later and broke out into the sun and fresh wind. A few dogged mosquitoes stayed with us all the way, but most of the skeeters — and nearly all the herons — had melted back into the sycamore jungle by the time we reached the water jug and the road home.

the unloved

American toad, with jack-in-pulpits in background. Note large parotid glands on "shoulders."

br'er toad's secret weapon

AN OLD HOP TOAD isn't a very mean customer. He doesn't have much in the way of muscles, almost nothing in the tooth and claw line, and isn't very bright. Except for being about the ugliest thing in sight, he doesn't bother anything but bugs.

He never looks for trouble, but when it comes he has several ways of handling it.

He can puff up with air to keep from being swallowed by a toad-eating snake, but this may not do much good because the hog-nosed snakes have special teeth for puncturing toads and deflating them to swallowing size. Or, he can feign death — playing 'possum with the best of them. But this may not help, either, for many critters like to eat dead things. Even dead toads.

A pestered toad may void urine, but some of the animals that are supposed to be offended by this don't really mind much.

But when things look blackest and everything else fails,

the toad still has a secret weapon in the warts that stud his back and sides.

These are actually small poison glands. When a hoptoad is *in extremis* he can contract the muscle fibers in these tiny glands and exude a milky fluid that is liquid fire to the mucus membranes of the mouths and eyes of most creatures, including man. You won't feel this poison's effects on your skin, but don't ever pick up a toad in your mouth!

This poison, contained in the largest quantity in the big parotid glands just behind the head, can cause temporary blindness in man and other mammals. It cannot, however, cause warts. Our most common toad, the American toad, isn't very big as toads go and has only a small amount of this poison at his command. Even so, a garden toad can cause a small animal to froth at the mouth or vomit.

There's a giant toad in Mexico that may measure $8\frac{1}{2}$ inches from stem to stern, and is pure poison all the way. It's been known to paralyze and kill dogs, and even men handle it with care. The venom of this enormous toad has been used for centuries by South American Indians as arrow poison. A couple of Johns Hopkins University scientists knew about this, and became interested in the various drug properties of toad venom.

John Abel and David Macht began working with exudates of the giant toad and isolated two important principles. One was a drug similar to those once used to stop bleeding and treat shock. The other was "bufagin," a substance that had properties similar to digitalis.

Modern workers with the National Heart Institute have continued these old investigations of toad venom with better equipment. According to Dr. Charles Bogert, Curator of Reptiles and Amphibians of the American Museum of Natural History, these new studies have uncovered still another valuable substance in toad venom. It is identical to *serotinin,* a material only recently found in human blood.

This stuff is evidently involved in the mechanism that

controls bleeding in the human body. Before discovering the material in toad venom, only tiny quantities of serotinin had been isolated from hundreds of tons of beef blood. Bogert says that in human beings it is held captive in the colorless discs in the blood called "platelets," but when injury ruptures the platelets this serotinin is released in minute quantities and causes the walls of the blood vessels to contract.

For the first time, serotinin is being made available in quantity from venom of the giant toad and is being used with radioactive materials to determine if it is involved in body processes that are upset during human disease.

It's no news that the toad, for all his ugliness, has been man's sidekick in the war against garden bugs. But it's a little startling to see him enlisted by pharmaceutics in a war against bugs we may never have seen.

A raft of predacious water beetles, family **Gyrinidae**.

waterbugs

YOU'RE NOT ALONE, fishing. Skating around your bobber on the quiet water are water striders, and that commotion on the inlet is their cousins — the backswimmers and water boatmen.

Those water striders are true bugs, spider-like children of the great insect order *Hemiptera* and first cousins to the bedbugs and chinch bugs.

Skating aimlessly around the surface of the pond, the water striders live on the incredibly thin film created by the surface tension of water particles. This film, or "neuston," is a world in itself, supporting a community of peculiar citizens. As in our world, the most successful residents are specialized. Some occur only on the bottom of the surface film, some live in it, and others — like the striders — are associated with the roof of this thin, tough film.

Water striders are the lions of the neuston, preying on dead and living insects that fall into the water. When times are tough, they may leap out of the water to capture flying insects. The undersurfaces of their bodies and long, slender legs are covered with a dense pile that keeps them absolutely dry. They're independent little bugs, and some species of water striders have been found in the ocean hundreds of miles from land.

Their cousins, the backswimmers, are the little black and white darting insects that paddle along the water's surface or just beneath it. They swim on their backs, which are keeled like boats.

The bellies of these insects have two double rows of fine hairs, each enclosing a small furrow that traps a pocket of air. When the backswimmer dives he takes his own air down with him in a sort of low level SCUBA arrangement.

A pair of long, fringed and flattened legs kick the backswimmer at a strong clip through the water. These bugs are predacious, feeding on small insects, crustacea, and sometimes even small fish. Their sucking beaks can inflict a severe sting; I once took a jolt at the base of my forefinger that I felt all the way to the elbow. In the dim old days when swimsuits were swimsuits and women were women (although men weren't always sure of it) backswimmers sometimes became entangled in bathing garb and used ladies badly. This is no longer a problem.

Water boatmen are gray and black mottled bugs less than a half-inch long that also have a pair of long, flattened legs. They swim with a swift, darting motion and when diving usually encase their bodies with an air bubble that makes them look as if they'd been plated with silver. Underwater, they must cling to objects to stay there, for this air supply would otherwise bob them to the surface. In stagnant water they come up regularly to recharge their air supply, but in fresh water their air bubble is replenished by air particles in the water. Not as predacious as their relatives, they scoop up most of their food from the bottom ooze with spoon-like mouthparts.

Down Mexico way these water boatmen are "farmed." They like to lay their eggs on a certain type of water grass. The *indios* tie this grass together in large bundles and float it on the surface of a pond until it is covered with water boatmen eggs. The bundles of grass are taken from the water and beaten over ground cloths until the eggs loosen and fall away. The eggs are then cleaned and powdered into flour.

They say it's nourishing. Care for more tortillas?

the turtle hunters

IT WAS EARLY JUNE and for ten days the south fork of the Skunk had been in full flood, drowning the bottomlands around Coons' Honey Stand and below Sig Olsen's place. But now the river was dropping back into its channel, leaving broad silt slicks where the eddies had been, and the river creatures were resuming their normal routines.

There was a big new mudbar about ninety yards below the bluff top where I lay in the thin shade of the new hickory leaves. It was down there, two days before, that we had seen the heavy drag marks of a very large snapping turtle and had waited vainly for hours for a glimpse of the reptile.

But this time, as I bellied up to the brink of the bluff, I could see the grayish, mud-caked shell of the turtle fully fifty feet from the water. There was no possibility of getting any closer, but I had foreseen this and had come heeled with what was surely the most terrible express rifle in my small world — a venerable .30-40 Krag carbine that I sometimes scrounged from Tom Sheesley for Very Big Hunts.

Keeping my eyes on the distant turtle, I settled the old rifle into position, depressed the muzzle until the sight blade bisected the turtle's carapace, and squeezed that creepy abomination of a military trigger. The ancient cartridge detonated and a gout of mud erupted just above the turtle.

The big snapper began stumping off to the water. Suddenly it became a croc making for the Zambesi with my best gunbearer in its jaws, and I was a vengeful Trader Horn. The old Krag boomed and leaped, abusing my thin shoulder, and at the fifth shot the turtle executed a leisurely, slow-motion flip.

Feeling like the hero in a 1939 movie, I lowered the fuming rifle and eyed the battle-torn mudbar and the defunct turtle, which was lying on its back weakly waving its legs. Stitched neatly across the mud were four gallon-deep craters marking my misses, but I justified these with the persuasion that — after all — the turtle had been on a dead run.

Then there was a hail from beyond the fence. The farmer who owned the land came legging it toward me, pretty disturbed at hearing a big-bore rifle salvoing in the middle of his stock range.

"Kid, just what do you think *you're* doing?" he yelled.

Feeling less like Trader Horn, and more like a skinny adolescent, I mumbled: "Shot a turtle."

"How's that? You shot a *what?*" he stormed. That was a mad farmer, all right.

"Shot a big snapper down there on the mud," I said lamely, pointing.

The farmer squinted down at the distant mudbar for a moment and turned to me. His face wasn't as red as it had been.

"Blamed if you didn't, at that. Big old snapper. What you gonna do with it, kid?"

"Oh, I don't know — make something out of its shell, mebbee."

"You don't want the meat?"

"No, sir."

"Well, then. I'll just have it my ownself," he said, and started down the face of the bluff, slipping and sliding.

I stood there and watched while he gobbed across the mudbar to the turtle, picked it up and hefted it, and started back toward the bluff. By the time he had gotten back on top, I was long gone.

That was my first brush with a dedicated turtle man.

Until then, I had regarded turtles as worthy rifle targets, and nothing more. I didn't care much for snapping turtles then, and I still don't. Relics of a younger world, they haven't gotten any prettier in a hundred million years, and there's a look of ancient evil about their tiny, star-pupilled eyes, heavy necks, and frightful mouths. They are the tyrannosaurs of the modern turtles, impressive in power and malevolence. Some large species are capable of chopping off a man's hand with their horny, toothless jaws.

I have learned since, however, that ugliness — like beauty — is only skin deep and that the snapping turtle's rough exterior hides some very fine rations. I've also learned that the best time to hunt turtles isn't in summer, but in late fall or even winter, and that the most effective turtle-getter isn't the rifle but a five-foot steel probe.

When the rivers and ponds of our upper midwest begin to chill in mid-October, snapping turtles dig in for the winter. They are ectothermic animals, dependent on outside sources for their body heat, and their chemistry slows in proportion to dropping temperatures. As the water temperature dips toward sixty degrees, the turtles grow sluggish and stiff. They dig into the soft mud of creek bottoms and marsh basins, their metabolisms greatly decelerate and they absorb their tiny oxygen requirements through the walls of their rectums.

Once the turtles have dug in, hardbitten specialists hunt

them with slender steel rods with sharpened ends, one end bent into a hook. These hunters wade slowly in small creeks, probing into the mud below the water's edge, covering maybe fifteen feet a minute and probing every eight or ten inches along the shoreline. If a hard object is struck and "rings," it is surely a rock. If the object is soft and punky, it may be a buried log or stump. But if the steel probe telegraphs an audible "thunk" preceded by a muffled "slurp," you're on target!

The "slurp" is a signal that you've broken into the pocket of air that may be trapped by the collapse of the turtle's entrance burrow. When the wall of this air pocket is ruptured, it can sometimes be heard, and an old turtle hunter may say that he's "busted the seal."

The "thunk," of course, is the steel rod tip punching against the shell of a buried turtle.

By repeated probing, you can determine the periphery of a turtle's carapace and estimate the reptile's size. The rod is then reversed and the sharp hook on the other end is shoved into the mud, engaged in the edge of the shell, and the weakly protesting turtle is wrenched out of the mud.

There's always a protest. I have never seen a hooked turtle that was completely dormant, even when pulled out of a spring seep into air with thirty degrees of frost. It comes out of its bed as a fetid mass of mud, with legs waving and jaws gaping and snapping stiffly. Sometimes — when a turtle is buried amid the root tangles of a creekside cottonwood — it may seize a deep root and grip doggedly with powerful jaws, and it can be a two-man job to disinter a five-pound snapper. In unobstructed mud, however, even large turtles can be easily pulled out of bed.

Only once have I hooked a turtle that resisted every effort to dislodge it. This was a solitary old-timer and we had found no smaller turtles in the immediate area — a tipoff that this was a lunker. There were no roots or obstructions in the mud, but the big snapping turtle was covered by nearly three feet of viscous mud. I socked the turtle hook solidly into the edge of the carapace, but the reptile refused to budge even when we pulled hard enough to tear away part of his upper shell — a plate of bone as large as a man's palm. I've always regretted not being able to raise that snapper. It must have been an imposing beast, for I've helped pull out twenty-five-pounders that gave way with comparative ease.

Very large snapping turtles appear to hibernate in solitude; smaller turtles often winter in groups. These mid-sized snappers may be stacked in the mud like cookies, four or five deep, and may even be tipped on edge. I once saw a turtle hunter probe and hook nine snapping turtles without moving from his tracks.

Most of my turtling has been in small pasture creeks six or eight feet wide. Such creeks are seldom too deep to wade, and turtles seem to hang out in the mud just below the water's edge where they can be easily found. Larger streams have their turtles, too; but they are not easily hunted, for the turtles there are not restricted to confined areas.

Until I met Bill Kunkle and his pretty wife Eileen, I'd never hunted turtles after freezeup.

In even the cruelest winter there are pasture drainages and spring seeps that never close. Bill and Eileen watch for such places in the barren, windswept prairies of western Iowa and regularly hunt turtles in midwinter.

It cost me a fifty-cent bet one cold December day to see how they do it. Bill, Eileen, their daughter Barbara and I walked across a bleak pasture to a small, boggy seep that never froze. Fed by a drain tile and deep springs, it was a maze of small channels and bottomless mud that was fenced to protect livestock from miring. In twenty minutes the Kunkles had hooked me and five snapping turtles, pocketed my four bits, and were on their way home.

Like all turtle hunters, Bill and Eileen eat the turtles they catch. I've never known a bona fide turtle hunter who

In the soft mud of a spring seep the huntress feels for a buried turtle with her steel probe. Reversing the rod she pushes the hooked end into the mud, snags the edge of the turtle's shell and pulls!

(opposite page)
On family turtle hunts guess who is left holding the bag. Unafraid of the vicious snappers, the young lady coolly pops them into a burlap sack and brings them back alive.

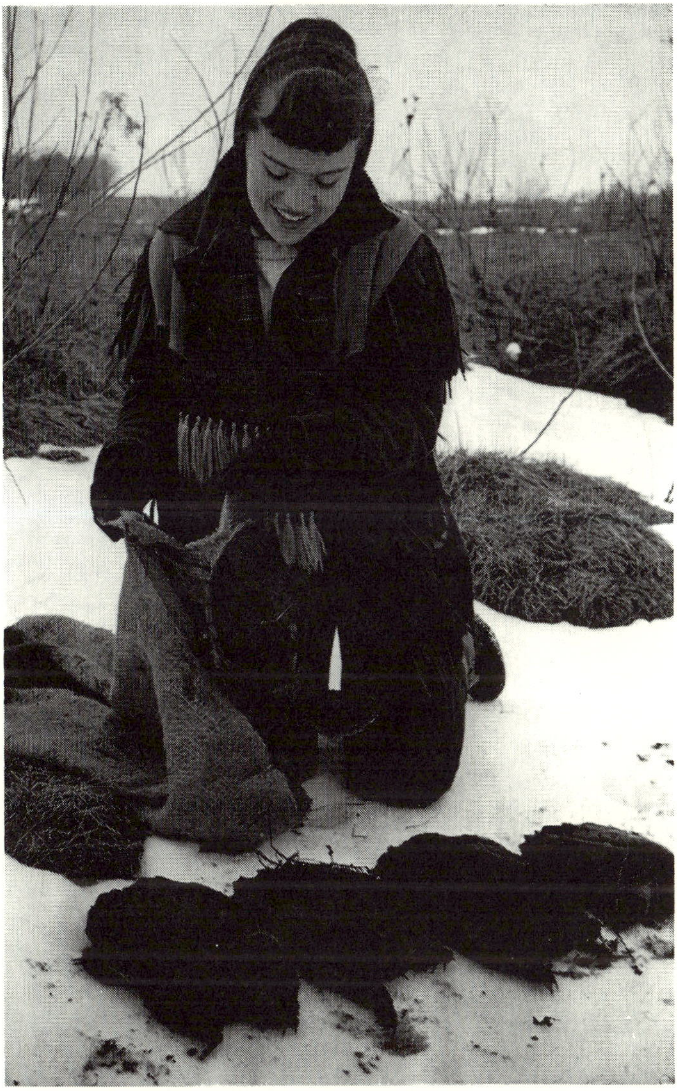

didn't consider it a top sport, or didn't relish turtle meat.

Only the neck and legs are kept for food, although a strip of tenderloin inside the upper shell may also be eaten. With a hatchet you cut away the plastron and carapace, skin the legs and neck, cut off all fat, and soak the lean meat in salt water for several hours. Then you roll it in flour, fry it like chicken until brown, and top it off in a hot oven for a couple of hours. Properly cooked, the meat is delicious.

It makes good soup, too, especially in the spring when the big females are carrying eggs. These eggs work into the turtle soup pretty well, and so do a few wild leeks in early spring. There's nothing puny about proper turtle soup.

There used to be five guys from Ohio who would drive out to a little Iowa town every summer for a week of turtle hunting. They did it the hard way, hand-grabbing snapping turtles from the muskrat holes and snags of nearby creeks. A risky business, but if they were badly bitten now and then, they didn't let on. Wading slowly, they would grope barehanded in the muddy depths, and when they felt a big turtle they'd simply haul him out of his lair. At the end of the week they would take over a local café, pay the cook a bonus, and feed turtle to most of the town.

After that, their pickup truck laden with the remaining snappers, the men would vanish into the east as suddenly as they had appeared. This went on for several years, and grew into a small local tradition that the townsfolk regarded with the sort of pride that they might have shown in a three-headed calf or a champion beer-drinker.

But one year the turtle expedition failed to show, never to return, and the community settled back to normal summers of fried catfish and homemade ice cream. There was some desultory discussion of the matter around town, but only one conclusion was ever drawn: that Ohio turtle-grabbers were certainly strong-willed men, but were helpless to prevail against the vacation plans of their wives.

beware the paper cities!

MY MORBID ATTRACTION to bugs that bite and sting may stem from that day on Squaw Creek nearly thirty years ago when I was sitting on the bank watching Moon Hansen execute "suckup" dives into a deep eddy.

About all I was wearing was freckles, and I had my bare legs draped over the brink of the creek bank. Somewhere in that creek bank was a nest of yellow-jacket wasps. It was early summer when such wasps have a notoriously low boiling point, especially when a small, naked boy is drumming against their doorway with his heels.

The deep water was only about seven feet below me, but that flight through the air seemed a lot longer than it really was. A dozen of the wasps took me on the wing, and I hit the water in full whoop in what was easily the most spectacular dive of the day. After a while the older boys poulticed me with cool mud, the stings swelled up grandly, and I was very brave. To this day — when someone mentions wasps — I feel the quiet heroism that comes from suffering well-borne, and a lingering regret that wasp stings don't leave scars. I deserved at least that much.

There was another day, years later, when I thought I'd achieved those scars. It was early in the squirrel season. I was crawling under a barbed wire fence when a lone yellow-jacket slipped under my shirt collar. He was where I couldn't reach him, and before I got to my feet I thought he'd cut me in half.

Yellow-jackets are potent from either end. Their powerful jaws are capable of chewing fence posts and can cruelly abuse the tender pelt between a man's shoulders. Alternately biting and stinging, that wasp stitched me fiercely before I came up yelling from under the fence and got to a tree to rub my back against. That night the mirror showed a trail of red welts extending ten inches across my back. I didn't feel heroic about this episode — only indignant. Somehow, being stabbed in the back while bellying under a fence smacks of dirty pool.

Bees have painful stings, but they're one-shot warriors. Their stingers are barbed and cannot be withdrawn once they're inserted. When a stinging bee is brushed away, its stinger tears out of the abdomen and ruptures delicate organs, invariably killing the insect. But wasps and hornets carry unbarbed spears and they can strike repeatedly and with impunity.

Only the females have stingers — small, polished lancets of chitin that were originally intended for egg-laying. In other insects these ovipositers are inserted into the ground or into plant stems and act as guides for the emerging eggs. In the wasps, hornets and bees this delicate spine has evolved to a highly specialized weapon connected with two large poison sacs and is no longer used for egg-laying.

This venom contains a potent charge of formic acid. The severity of the sting depends largely on the quantity and concentration of the acid and other agents. Stingers are used for defense by bees, but they are offensive weapons with the predacious wasps and hornets who feed on insects that are paralyzed or killed by the stings.

Even more ferocious than the yellow-jacket is that black and white thunderbolt, the bald-faced hornet. It may be over an inch long, totally black except for white markings on the abdomen and a white patch on the face and head.

Beware! Several bald hornets, surprised at work on their unfinished nest, threaten the photographer.

No other stinging insect in North America can match it. I would rather surprise a basking rattlesnake than a nest of bald hornets in early summer.

This is the creature that builds the great paper nests — sometimes as large as bushel baskets — found in the trees and bushes of the back country. With their hard, strong jaws, the hornets scrape fine wood shavings from weathered posts and dead trees, moistening the shavings with saliva. This tiny wad of wet wood pulp is carried back to the nest site and extruded in a thin ribbon on the outside of the growing nest where it hardens and dries to become gray paper. Yellow-jackets build similar nests underground, usually near water. Bald hornets suspend their nests in the open, where they were once found by early settlers and used as wadding for muzzle-loading shotguns.

The nest is begun by the queen hornet, the only one to survive the winter. After hibernating in an old stump or punky log, she emerges at the first signs of warm weather. At the end of a paper stalk hung beneath a branch or strong twig, the queen constructs several small cells and lays a single egg in each. These hatch to become sterile female workers that obediently begin building their queen's palace. When these young workers mature, the queen retires and devotes her time to egg-laying. The workers diligently scrape wood for their monarch, make paper, enlarge the nest and build more cells into which the queen lays more eggs to hatch more workers, *ad infinitum*.

The hit-or-miss feeding of the large number of grubs, especially when food is scarce in spring, results in poorly-nourished larvae. Some scientists believe that this malnutrition is responsible for the undeveloped sex organs that cause many female hornets to be sterile. Since these insects are never occupied with reproduction, their lives are consumed by two ends — working and fighting. They become amazons — the warriors of the swarm. Later in the season, when food is more abundant, the larvae are better fed and grow to be fully developed fertile males and females.

By summer's end the queen hornet has mothered several thousand workers, some males, and a few young queens. There may be seven tiers of nest cells in the great paper structure, and as many as 10,000 hornets. With the coming of cold weather the workers and males die and the nest is deserted. The immense labor, sound and fury of the paper city is to achieve but one end — the production of a few fertile queens to perpetuate the race.

While bald hornets are engaged in all this nest-building and family-rearing they are very touchy. Always on the prod, they become incredibly vicious at this time and may dive-bomb a passing fisherman for no apparent reason. Since they are so large, and occur in such great numbers, these attacks can be extremely serious.

They seem to center their assaults on a man's face, particularly in the region of the forehead and eyes. They may attack any large animal within twenty feet of their nest, slamming into the unhappy target at top speed, business-end first. The impact of this attack often kills the hornet, and it's a shock that will always dwell in a man's memory. It seems incredible that an insect can actually stagger a man or boy, but there have been enough accounts of this to warrant some basis in fact. It probably isn't the physical impact that jolts a man, but the fact that the attack is centered on his sensitive facial area.

Jack Musgrove, one of our favorite boondockers and brush-prowlers, told me of such an encounter. He was once shooting a large paper nest of bald hornets with a slingshot when he suddenly found himself sitting down. His first thought was that his slingshot fork had snapped and that the broken crotch had smashed into his face. What had really hit him was one of the big hornets in a full power dive, catching him fairly between the eyes.

"How did it feel?" I asked him one day.

"Well. . . I can't really say," Jack replied. "I've never felt anything like that before."

"Was it something like getting hit with a club? That's what I've heard."

"No-o-o," Jack said thoughtfully. "Not like a club. It was sort of like getting hit with a hot pickaxe, if you know what I mean."

I didn't know what he meant, and I'm not about to find out. Since that day on Squaw Creek, I'll rest on my laurels.

the locks of medusa

Hunting poisonous snakes — whether for sport, profit, or out of some dim sense of ancestral outrage — is a tense affair.

When you go into snake country with the sober intent of capturing venomous serpents, there is a tendency to walk with both feet off the ground and to find yourself wishing for galvanized pants. You are drawn to an almost painful tautness, especially if you are bent on taking the snakes alive. You'll never be sharper. Perceptions that have been overlaid by a lifetime of civilized responses are suddenly bared and the human animal is its old, trembling self again, wanting to climb a tree.

Other sports are spiced with danger, but it's doubtful that any others have such unique overtones of horror. An Andalusian fighting bull or a Himalayan monsoon can inspire terror, but there is nothing like the dusty goblin's face of a coiled rattlesnake to inspire dread.

Most of my limited experience with poisonous reptiles

has been with the timber rattlesnake — a heavy-bodied pit viper usually found in wooded situations and especially in limestone country with its countless fissures and deep crevices. This snake winters deep in broken rock, sometimes in startling numbers. Its dens are often old established wintering places that have been used for thousands of generations.

During the first warm days of mid-spring when the sun stirs the rattlers' sluggish blood and draws them out into the balmy outer world, they may mass on ledges near these den entrances and sun themselves on the warm rock. This is one of the best times to hunt them, when there may be a dozen rattlers on a ledge no larger than a bathtub. As spring wears on the snakes will disperse to their hunting grounds in nearby woods and uplands, scattering through the thickening vegetation.

Most experienced snake hunters employ bent metal rods or "snake hooks" to gently lift the snakes into sacks or collecting cages. I have neither the savvy nor inclination to use such a hook; when I apprehend a rattlesnake I prefer to have it plumb demobilized. To this end, nothing is better than a short pole with a lanyard and a soft buckskin noose that can be slipped over the snake's head and drawn up snugly. The soft noose is necessary to prevent injury to the reptile, for few creatures are more delicate. If the snake is a heavy one, it may even be necessary to support his body while lifting him from the ground in order to prevent spinal damage.

Rattlesnake hunting is usually unspectacular, for these vipers are shy animals that seldom exhibit any pyrotechnics. They are dangerous only when badly startled, injured, or subjected to indignities that even snakes cannot be expected to tolerate. They are rarely aggressive in the human sense and even though they hold a whip hand over most wild creatures, they are not bullies. There have been cases where rats placed in rattlesnake cages as food have turned on the rattlers and killed them.

Although they are always unpredictable, I have never seen rattlesnakes strike without provocation, and for nastiness and sheer cussedness the common water snakes are far uglier to handle. It is not unusual to walk within inches of coiled rattlers that never strike, and such snakes may not even buzz.

Two of us were once collecting timber rattlers in an abandoned limestone quarry and stopped to rest on a low outcropping. We discussed our plan of action and argued our next move. When we had finished our smokes we continued down the old narrow-gauge track that we had been following. About fifty yards up the track we abruptly changed our minds and turned back the way we had come, passing the ledge where we had been sitting five minutes before. As we walked by the rocky overhang and viewed it from a slightly different angle, I glimpsed the sooty glow of thick coils beneath it. In the mouth of the crevice was the largest timber rattlesnake either of us had ever seen, and about two feet away from its flat, spade-shaped head was my cigarette butt. My legs had been within easy striking range of the snake, probably for as long as I had sat there, but the reptile had made no move to attack and had not even sounded its nervousness. We tried vainly to noose the snake in the cramped space under the ledge, but it slid safely back into its lair and we parted company.

Much the same thing, but with another species of pit viper, occurred last summer beside one of our favorite Ozark swimming holes — a very fine little pool rimmed with a narrow, sandy beach that is littered with great boulders and outcroppings.

Several families had been playing around that pool all morning. Children and adults were all over the place until

A timber rattlesnake — cocked and ready. Note the elliptical eye pupil that is characteristic of all pit vipers.

shortly before noon when a light rain began and everyone cut for their tents and cars. Several of us were just preparing to leave when someone saw a large copperhead under an outcropping of porphyry at the edge of the small beach. We didn't know how long the snake had lain there, but if it had been there for more than fifteen minutes it had been within a few inches of bare feet at least a dozen times. I bashed the snake but with none of my usual snake-bashing spleen, for it was a beautiful thing and showed absolutely no inclination to mischief.

Only once have I had a pit viper deliberately press home an attack.

I had noosed this big timber rattler on a mossy bench at the base of a rock wall fifty feet above a river. It was a splendid specimen, newly-rid of its old skin and shining like a new penny. The snake was loosely coiled and unexcited when the buckskin strap dropped over it, but raised its head abruptly just as I tightened the noose. The snake was caught too far down the neck, and had been partly lifted from the ground when it began striking at a knot of the slip cord. Fearing injury to the rattler's mouth, I slacked the noose slightly to allow the strap to slip up snugly behind its flaring jaws. But I loosened the strap too much. The snake's head slipped through the noose and the reptile fell heavily to the ground. It coiled at once, struck on reflex as I leaped back, formed an S without coiling, and immediately struck again.

There was little doubt that this snake was on the prod — albeit defensively — but it "cooled off" quickly in the cage and gave no further trouble. I also cooled off, and still feel a chill when I recall how close my second backward jump brought me to the edge of the bluff.

For all their lethargy and general indisposition to join battle, rattlesnakes are potent animals.

The hypodermic fangs of a rattler inject a haemotoxic venom — a highly-modified saliva — that attacks red blood cells, the walls of capillaries and, to a much lesser degree, the nervous system. Such a bite is excruciating, and its danger is proportional to the size of the snake, the bulk of its victim, and the depth and location of the venom injection. Only once have I seen the effects of a rattlesnake bite, and they were quite impressive.

A young Mexican laborer had been struck on his inner forearm while picking vegetables on a truck farm near Tucson. The bite was almost certainly that of a western diamondback rattlesnake. Ligation had been applied to the man's arm above the elbow, but the tourniquet had not been administered properly, no incisions had been made to drain the bite area, and medical treatment was delayed for at least three hours. The man was incoherent, in great pain, and his arm was terribly swollen. The flesh in the vicinity of the wound was a blackened, pulpy swelling of alarming proportion — a characteristic of rattlesnake venom which breaks down the tissue and floods it with broken blood. Aside from the immediate effects of the deadly venom, there is always danger of serious secondary infection.

By the time the young Mexican arrived for treatment he was burning with fever. He was given massive injections of rattlesnake antivenin and a long series of blood transfusions. Both his life and arm were saved — no thanks to the half-dozen hysterical kinsmen who had tried their own faith cures before seeking medical help.

At the other extreme is my friend Frank Heidelbauer, who was struck in the knee by a small copperhead while climbing out of a Pennsylvania trout stream.

Frankie knew what to do and did it. He killed the snake, upped his pant's leg, and got busy with his knife. When the wound was bleeding freely and a tourniquet was knotted about his thigh, Frank hobbled to his car and hied himself to the nearest doctor.

When the wound was dressed, the doctor told Frank: "That snake didn't do you any good, but it wasn't nearly as hard on your knee as you were. What did you incise this snakebite with . . . a circle saw?"

In some states, rattlesnake hunting may be a commercial operation with bounties as high as fifty cents per snake being paid by county auditors who demand proof-on-payment of the snake's head, or its rattles attached to two inches of tail. If the snake's head is required, there is no doubt of the reptile's demise. But in a few states, only the rattles and two inches of tail constitute proof of a dead rattlesnake and a vicious and dangerous bounty dodge has been developed.

Dead snakes don't increase their tribe, and near-extermination of rattlers could dry up a source of back-country revenue. So in a sort of left-handed conservation measure, a few snake hunters may capture rattlers alive, cut off the rattles and required two inches of tail, and release the pain-maddened reptiles to roam the countryside. If such snakes survive, there's no reason to believe that they would behave normally. Aside from not being able to produce any sort of warning, these mutilated rattlers might be excessively edgy, and one can hardly blame them.

A more humane bounty dodge is to simply keep a few gravid female rattlers in a barrel until they give birth to their living young, and then bounty the entire brood.

For the record, I have no first-hand knowledge of either of these bounty gyps. However, I have a very low esteem of bounties in general and I don't have the slightest doubt that such hoaxes have been — and are still being — perpetrated on ingenuous county auditors.

So far as I know, Joe Martelle has always played it straight. Snake hunting is only one of a battery of Martelle vocations that includes clam-fishing, mink-trapping, cutting staves for whiskey barrels, and gandydancing. His county auditor pays him fifty cents for every rattlesnake that he kills and "proves on." In a slack season Joe will haunt the rocky hillsides above Harper's Ferry and play hob with the timber rattler population. In a week or so, he may pick off fifty or sixty rattlesnakes, and while a man won't get rich at a half-dollar per snake, it tides him over until the river rises or the railroad starts hiring section hands.

Most areas in snake country have local "Rattler Ridges" or "Snake Hills," and the land behind Harper's Ferry is no exception. This is a place where the land stands on its hind legs and shows its limestone muscles, a rough, wild, wooded region that is prime rattlesnake country.

There's a broad, open hillside above Little Paint Creek — a southerly slope that is strewn with stunted cedars and seamed with limestone ledges — that is particularly fertile snake habitat. I have never prowled that hillside in summer without seeing rattlers, and it is one of Joe's favorite hunting areas. He roams that hillside and the high ridges that flank it with a stick and a sack. When he sees a basking rattlesnake he simply steals up on it and swats it like a fly, at fifty cents a swat.

There is a tenet that old snake hunters — like old powder monkeys — often develop a fatal lack of caution. But pro that he is, Joe never takes chances. When he is working on a "hot" rattler he buzzes almost as much as the snake. One day, while I was transferring a live rattlesnake to a sack Joe was holding, I noted that he held the sack at arm's length, face averted.

"What's the matter, Joe?" I teased. "You a little dauntsy about that snake?"

"When I don't r'ar back from a singing rattler," Joe said evenly, "you tell me about it. Because that's the day I worry about!"

Some men undoubtedly hunt rattlers out of unadorned hatred, or out of some atavistic drive that compels them to seek out and kill the things that they fear and dread the most. In many cases, rattlesnake hunting is simply the offbeat sport of the audacious thrill-seeker.

In Martelle's case — as with a few other snake hunters — it's simply a way of turning ready cash. But even Joe admits that it's a sticky way to earn four bits.

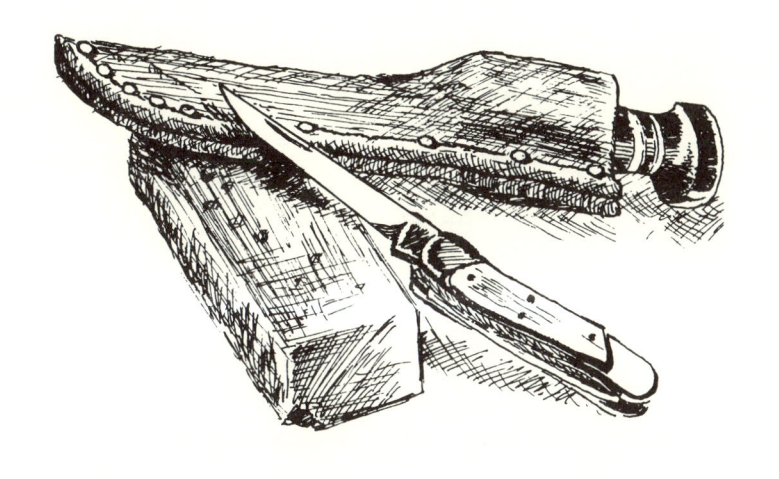

*short arrows
from the long bow*

the abashed savage

AMONG MODERN Americans there are two sharply divergent views of nature. At one pole is Thoreau, who declaims: "In wilderness is the preservation of the world." At the other is Helen Bell who, learning that a friend plans a walk in the country, quips: "Well, kick a tree for me."

My own view lies somewhere north of the equator. I incline strongly to the Thoreaus, but only to a point. For if I am outraged by sophisticates and their witty rejections of the natural world, I'm irked by the "Oh-the-wonder-of-it-all" school that includes most assistant scoutmasters, garden club ladies, poets at picnics, and the presumptuous asses who clutter perfectly good mountaintops with neon crosses.

From the leftist pole, I could never view nature with frivolity. She has chilled me too many times, baked me too often, and thrown her assorted rocks, lightnings and poison stings at me for too long to permit disrespect. Fear engenders respect, and I have spent enough time alone with nature to fear her and to accept my subordinate position.

There are a few who regard nature as a force in bondage, driven to its knees by an advanced human technology that has overcome the elemental obstacles of air, earth, fire and water. But man has shackled nothing but himself. The mischievous, ingenious imp has turned a few simple natural functions to his own ends and, as often as not, even these functions retaliate by killing or sickening him. He has sacrificed some of his most valuable animal gifts in his climb to dominance, yet remains subject to the biological checks which have always existed. Man may synthesize microclimates in which to polish his arts, but he remains forever subject to the great controls — disease, starvation, and interspecific and intraspecific strife — that dominate all biota.

From the liberal pole, I cannot regard nature with reverence in the accepted definition, and I'm puzzled by suburban transcendentalists who must rationalize a Sunday morning picnic as worship in the Great Green Church. The simple act of taking to the woods, on Sunday or otherwise, is testimony enough and needs no bowed head nor bent knee to sanctify it. In any case, the infusion of wild nature into tame religion smacks of hypocrisy, for no western religion today actively defends or apparently understands what some ecclesiastics blandly call "God's Wild Wonders."

Nor can I regard nature with any particular affection, nor understand clubwomen who gush: "I simply *adore* Mother Nature!"

Adoration is as alien to wild nature as blasphemy. Nature transcends love, goodness, malevolence or evil. It is simply a primordial force — shining, aloof and brooding, a vast sweep of power too awful to be imbued with human emotions, virtues or mischiefs. It is as presumptuous to adore nature as it is to kick a redwood.

At one pole, the poets and the Spartan Scoutmaster of Walden Pond. At the other, the darling of the Back Bay parlors and her bright, synthetic retinue.

And somewhere in between, several million of us awed, abashed savages who wonder at lightning and the flight of the crane, and who walk in the open world because we are not content to walk elsewhere, and because it is the only real home — however mystic and terrifying — that we shall ever know.

snake liars

OF ALL the unvarnished liars in this world, the snake liar is the worst.

It's pretty hard to beat a fishing liar or a grizzly-hunting liar, unless you ring in a long-range-duckshooting liar. But all of them have to go some to beat a good snake liar.

I'd always thought I'd heard some fancy snake liars in my time, but I met one awhile back in the Louisiana bayou country who shaded them all. We were just talking about fishing and getting along all right when this gent gave me a slaunchwise look and started in to lie.

"Mister," he says. "You know anything about snakes?"

"A little."

"Well, a little won't git it," he says. "Now you set, and I'm gonna tell you about snakes."

He sure did. That man sat there and ripped into some of the most shameless snake stories you ever heard. He wasn't just fibbing, either, like we all do when we talk fishing. He was flat-out *lying*, this man was.

He said he'd been struck as a boy by a cottonmouth that weighed fifty pounds. Coiled, that snake was bigger than a bushel basket. When it struck, it tore away the left half of my host's face, but the healing qualities of an absinthe and crayfish bisque diet were such that this didn't even leave a scar.

From there we went to "stumptails" — some sort of varmint that's only ten inches long but has a fist-sized head and a body as thick as a stevedore's forearm.

Then we got around to rattlesnakes.

"Biggest rattler I ever seen in these parts," he said, watching me for any flicker of disbelief, "was killed 'way back in the cane when I was a tad. Big around as a jointed stovepipe, that snake was, and fourteen foot long by actual measure and with thutty-two rattles by actual count."

He paused to let me chew on that.

"We never did find out how much that sarpint weighed, but my daddy hitched a horse to it and drug it out of the cane like a lawg. Just like a great big ol' pi'zen lawg!"

The clincher was one about a snake that could coil on the surface of a bayou as if it were dry land, and strike at passing boats.

"I've had a hunnerd of them strike my pirogue," my host said, "and sometimes the cypress swole around the place that was snake-bit!"

Now, this man was sincere and didn't mean any mischief. Snake liars just can't help themselves; there's something about snakes that *obliges* them to lie. And so we have Snake Stories — rich stews of outdoor fancy that are sparingly seasoned with facts and brought to their full flavor by years of telling.

We could probably do without snake liars, but things wouldn't be the same. Take the fire-breathing dragons of the fairy tales, for instance. Thought up by old-time snake liars, every one of them!

When you look at it that way, it makes a difference, for what would childhood be without dragons? It wouldn't surprise me if the snake liars of today are the Brothers Grimm of tomorrow, and maybe the Story of the Slithery Stumptail will fascinate children long after they've become bored with space travel and lunar playgrounds.

the little sports

WHEN THE BASS go off their feed or the squirrel hunting slows down, I turn to the little sports.

They aren't much, but I've never managed to outgrow them and they give me homey comfort when I have time on my hands. I mean small excursions for such stuff as nightcrawlers, softshell crawdads, mushrooms, arrowheads, and perfect slingshot forks.

It's a tough choice, but of all these things — even above morel mushrooms — I think I lean to arrowheads and perfect slingshot forks.

I've prowled a thousand leagues of muddy fields but have yet to find a perfect, unbroken arrowhead. Bushels of chips and broken points and pottery shards and such truck. But never a perfect point. After years of consistent failure and near misses, I can't help but think that the red gods are saving me for something special. Like maybe a chalcedony lancehead or an agate amulet.

Oh, I've come close.

There was the time on a bluff above the Boone River when I saw a shining jasper splinter nearly buried in the dirt at the base of a white oak. I could even see one of the delicately carved notches where sinew once lashed the point to a lance shaft. I carefully unearthed the find; it had been snapped in two, perhaps by the last man to use it.

Then there was the rodman on my old surveying crew who wandered down into the woods during his lunch hour. He walked directly to a limestone overhang, reached underneath, and gathered a peck of perfect arrowpoints that had been cached there by some ancient arrowsmith.

A few years ago Paul Kline and I were walking in plowed fields one spring afternoon. Paul is a game biologist, a splendid amateur archaeologist, and one of the sharpest field men I've ever met. We studied some likely ground that day, found many broken points and flakes, and Paul's quiet stories fanned my old fires.

In mid-afternoon, while walking fifty feet apart through a newly-plowed field, Paul suddenly stopped and called to me. I walked over to him and looked down at the raw loam at his feet.

The flawless arrowpoint was completely exposed, lying in the black soil as if it had been dropped minutes before. It was a Hopewell point flaked from a nodule of white chert — a delicate fragment of neolithic culture that had been shaped during a primitive Renaissance. Thin and perfect in its symmetry, with razor edges sweeping down in curved arcs to the incredibly sharp point, this was one of the pieces carried to the far tribes by Hopewellian priests. Here was no crude flint splinter roughly shaped to fit in a split stick. This was taste and grace, created in pride and carried by men of religious fervor — mystic artisans of a culture that dawned too late and faded too soon.

I knew Paul wanted that point for his collection, and I wanted him to have it. After all, he'd found it. But I asked him to let me pick it up.

I was the first man to touch that weapon for possibly ten centuries. The last man to touch it before me had surely known what he had, and I was handling the same arrowpoint and sharing his pride in it. I had bridged ten thousand years and had nodded congratulations to a Stone Age man. The red gods had let me get my foot in the door. . . .

My slingshots are an incurable hangover from a youth when juvenile delinquents were simply real boys. In those old, sweet days of perpetual sunshine and hungry catfish, a slingshot was the only logical treatment for cats, cows, bottles, street lights, sparrows and rabbits. Not to mention the odd windowpane.

Today I tote a slingshot for basking turtles and crazy bird dogs. And because I've never quite outgrown slingshots, I am still in the market for perfect forks.

It's cheating if you saw your own fork out of a board. You must find one, ready-shaped by nature, in a tree. The best come from boxelder and green ash, trees with scads of symmetrical forks that anyone can find. But I'm a purist and for a quarter-century I have sought the golden fleece — a walnut slingshot fork of faultless symmetry.

Like the unbroken arrowhead quest, this search has been fruitless. I don't suppose I'll ever find such a fork, for walnut trees just don't grow that way. But to this day I can't pass up a likely walnut grove and I claim to have shinnied up more walnut trees than any living person over twelve years old, and most squirrels. No luck yet, but I'm still trying.

However, I've grown pretty handy at fork-hunting — the smallest of the little sports. And someday, graying hair and all, I may be the luckiest kid in my neighborhood with a perfect, hand-polished, genuine black walnut slingshot.

On the famous Kalsow Prairie north of Manson, Iowa, young Dale Jones and his sisters, Becky and Martha, romp in a patch of bluestem grass just as children of the pioneers once did. This photograph was taken in August when the prairie was a patchwork of color, when the big bluestem waved higher than a man's head, and little bluestem and buffalo grass rippled in the summer wind. In this living link with the past, a child can hide all day and dream of Indians.

a wilderness of light

NOT SO LONG AGO, between the eastern forests and the buffalo plains, there was a sea of grass and flowers.

The midland of the continent was open, rolling, long-grass prairie and settlers emerging from the woods and snug fields of the east were stunned by a blaze of sunlight and an immense sweep of sky.

The old settlers said it was like a sea with long, heavy groundswells. It was neither angular and abrupt nor flat and monotonous, but a vast reach of grassland broken with stately groves and dissected by timbered stream valleys. One man wrote that where the groves crowded into the prairie the effect was like that of a rugged shoreline, with the surrounding forest indented to form bays and headlands in the grass and sometimes — when regarded across leagues of prairie — the distant forest was like "a dim shore beheld at a great distance from the ocean."

It was a unique, unliterary wilderness without pestilential swamps or black walls of forest. This was an open wilderness of birds, flowers, grass and sun. In the groves and timbered valleys were elk, deer, bear and turkey. On the open prairie were grouse beyond number and the eastern fringes of the great bison herds that blanketed the short-grass plains beyond the Platte.

A large land, whose breathtaking immensity of sky disturbed many travelers. It was this pitiless quality of *openness*, a relentless intimidation of wind and distance — even more than the marauding Sioux — that drove some settlers back to the east. It dwarfed them beyond their endurance and they fell back from this new land's largeness and its jarring excesses of light and space.

There was, and is, no other region in North America with such climatic extremes. With no large water bodies to temper the weather and no forests or mountains to check the wind, the prairie summers and winters were elemental entities, neither possessing any of the attributes of the other. The first storms of autumn might leave snow three feet deep on the level prairie and fill some sheltered ravines with drifts that lingered until early June. After the blizzards came weeks of bright, bone-cracking cold with seventy degrees of frost, only to be followed by a summer with blazing afternoons of a hundred and fifteen degrees and incessant winds that desiccated the prairies and their people and drove the great fires that consumed them both. Even if the settler survived winter, wildfire, sick oxen, renegade Wahpekutes, diphtheria and tetanus, there was still the aching loneliness and the prison of empty, illimitable horizons.

But it was worth it, and people crowded into the open land.

For never has there been such a place of incredible richness. This land had not invested its strength in trees, but had renewed and rebuilt itself annually as the lush prairie grasses and forbs had died and enriched the earth. There evolved a soil that was light, black and fluffy with organic matter. Even after the hardest rain and hottest sun, a man could walk over prairie loam and scuff his boots in it, and the soil was soft and flocky. It was much later, after the soil had been mined by decades of cash-grain farming, that it became as heavy and solid as the men who worked it.

Today the long-grass prairie is nearly gone, although

some scraps of it linger on a few farms, along old railroads, and in neglected country cemeteries. I know of only a few hundred-acre prairies in Iowa today, and these anachronisms are invariably ringed by farmers who eye them as wistfully and hungrily as orphans regard a jar of peppermints. Such men have fine farms and all the good land that they can comfortably manage, but they know that the keen edge of that land has been blunted by a century of cultivation. They ache to drill their modern seed into an ancient earth that has been storing up richness for ten thousand years.

The primeval soils of these prairies are also coveted by scientists. A few years ago a botanist with the Atomic Energy Commission told me that only virgin prairie areas can give chemists the patterns of our best original northern soils — patterns that will serve as reference indices in the event of atomic contamination of croplands. This could be vital, they say, in assaying the effects of atomic reactors and reactor wastes on soils and plants — and the atomic reactor age is upon us.

I'm too dull to be a farmer and too sharp to be an atomic scientist. But for reasons of my own I also prize the prairie, and am selfish enough to believe that those reasons are as good as any man's. I think we owe something to the life forms that have been hard-put to survive our technology, whether they be whooping cranes, prairies, or schoolteachers who spank.

One of my favorite places is a hundred and eighty acres of Iowa prairie that has never been plowed nor grazed. It has not been invaded by volunteer crop plants nor even exotic weeds, for the native prairie species are well-entrenched in their home sod and doggedly resist invasion. Except for a barn on the horizon and the fences that bar the covetous Holsteins and Herefords, the little patch of prairie is unchanged from the last ice age.

By late August, as I write this, that prairie is a grandmother's quilt of form and color. The ironweed is heavy with purple, flat-topped blooms and here and there are a few arrow-straight, magenta spikes of blazing-star. Most of the cornflowers are gone by this season, but you can see the rattlesnake-master with its spiny leaves and odd, bulbous seed heads and if you look carefully, you can find low shrubs of redroot with their huge, plow-busting, mahogany rootstocks.

There are wild grasses everywhere, the big bluestem waving higher than a man's head in lofty stands that were once cut for wild hay — a grass that makes the finest bedding for hunting dogs that I know of. There are open, sun-washed flats of little bluestem, dropseed grass and buffalo grass with the late summer wind running across them. Being in such a place is being in yesterday, and sometimes I can look across this prairie and feel my great-grandfather coming toward me, with his bullhide boots and linsey-woolsey breeches and walking with a two-furrow stride.

If you are a woman standing in that prairie, you can look at flowers that you have never seen before and may never see again. Think of a sod house with the nearest woman forty miles away; of hearing your children struggle with McGuffey's Reader by the light of bayberry candles.

If you are a man, walk out into this prairie and say: "I have just served in the war with Mexico, I was wounded at Churubusco, and Congress has given me this quarter-section as my land warrant."

If you are a small boy, find a soft place in a patch of yellow stargrass and dream of Injuns.

rivers

THERE'S LIFE and purpose to a river.

Lakes are fine but they never go anywhere; they just stay at home and sleep in their basins until they die. But a river goes on, and lives long. It likes to work, to ramble around and see what's beyond the next bend. It shouts, growls or sings songs, depending on how the country suits it. It may slow down and take a nap, or grow angry and throw its weight around. But whatever it does, it does with life and purpose.

There are many rivers, with many moods. There are the big ones like the Ohio and the Illinois — solid brown rivers, old, strong and deep, flowing deliberately and profoundly. There are the ones like Jack's Fork and the Black and the Buffalo, bright little streams filled with youth. Spring-fed, dancing over gravel beneath rock walls and cedar.

There are rivers with warbonnet names — the Nodaway, Niobrara, Wapsipinicon and Kaskaskia. Ones like the little desert stream in the foothills of the Chiracuhuas that Felix Khyatan showed me one blazing day, calling it some name in singing Apache. And if such names grow too stern and sonorous, there are the comic relief rivers named by white men: The Toad Suck, The Muddy Boggy, and Itch Crick.

My tastes in rivers change every few years. Right now I'm having an affair with the Mississippi, finest of the heavyweight rivers. The heart stream of the nation, successfully resisting the thromboses of the Army Engineers and the senseless embolisms of a million landowners along its watershed. A great, long-suffering river which, perhaps once a decade, swells with spring and thunders a Phillippic: "Dam *me*? Why, damn *you*!! I'm spreading out and moving on! Head for high ground or come along, it's all the same to me!" And the farm women weep, their men supplicate the Engineers, the Engineers make mighty pronouncements, and they all stand together on high ground and shake their fists at the brown giant below them.

I'll always admire the Mississippi. But in a few years, when my awe of strength begins to fade, I'll probably revert to the happiest streams of all — the creeks in the farm woodlots, their sun-dappled holes filled with such splendid things as small boys and sunfish, crawdads and cows. Places like the South Fork of the Skunk where I learned to cuss, smoke cornshuck cigarettes, and catch pumpkinseeds.

A man grows old and goes downstream to a bigger river, but he started from a headwater creek where it's always summer. And if he's blessed with total recall, and is as willing to forgive the changes in that headwater creek as in himself, he can come back upstream to home.

the unforgettable feists

LET'S TALK about hunting dogs. Not the blooded champs of stately grace and high birth, but those bandy-legged heroes of a million squirrel and rabbit hunts — the feists.

Webster defines *feist* as "a small dog." Properly, a hunting feist is a pup of tangled ancestry and nondescript coloring that is always found in the company of small boys and single-shot .22's.

There should be a special field trial class for such dogs. In such a competition, these should be judging points:

1. All good hunting feists are small, and yip. Authorities claim that the best hunting feist is never more than 12 or 15 inches at the shoulder. He should have a high, shrill voice and be happy to use it. He must be able to get under barns, corncribs, log piles, brush heaps, and into farm culverts and gooseberry thickets.

2. The hunting feist can go over, under or through barbed wire without being cut. While going to or from a hunt, the feist will often carry something in his mouth to relieve the boredom of travel. This may be a stick, a chunk of corncob or an old shotgun shell.

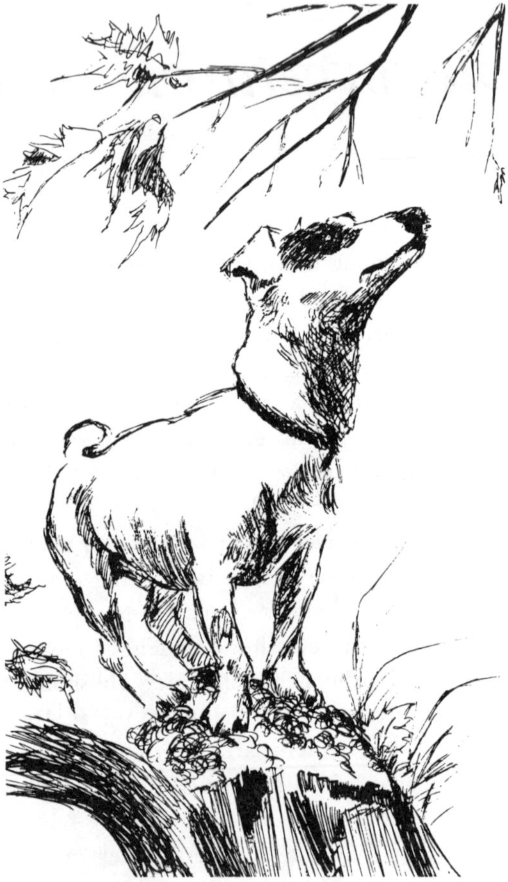

3. A likely hunting feist always trots on the bias. That is, when he's heading west his hinderparts are trailing somewhere in the southeast. As he runs he will hold one leg off the ground as if his foot is sore. His foot is not sore; the dog is simply saving it for later use, or something.
4. This dog must be able to swim, climb, dig and dodge expertly, and be happy to roll in carrion and hunt incessantly. He must be absolutely fearless. And every feist dog worth his gravy must be able to salute three posts out of every five, no matter how long the fence.

Color and shape are not important judging points, although it is preferable that a feist be low-slung and dirt-colored. You may choose from a vast variety of stripes, blotches and spots. The best breeds are usually obscure crosses of terriers, beagles, dachshunds, or anything else that happened along.

Because of this patchwork lineage, the hunting feist usually lacks the frantic timidity of some finely-bred gun dogs and is consistently loyal, rugged, healthy and calm.

Feists are superb squirrel and rabbit dogs, but they're good for hunting almost anything. They consider skunks personal insults that must be avenged at all costs. They'll tangle with turtles, groundhogs, goats, pigs, snakes and catfish. They will fight badgers into their dens and climb up inside hollow trees for big 'coons and 'possums. They are often whipped by such critters, but are never defeated.

These dogs are long remembered. Many hunters mistily recall their boyhood feists long after they've forgotten the blooded pointers and setters of manhood. That's because being a good gun dog isn't simply a matter of pastern, stifle and spring of rib. It's a matter of heart.

knife talk

"POKEY CHARLEY" Thompson was a leathery, dehydrated old prospector who had dug up the landscape from British Columbia to Sonora, and while he'd never found much color he certainly knew his way around.

We had been hunting javelinas in the Rincons and were sitting around after supper when Charley pointed at the fire with his pipe and said:

"There are three ways to peg an outdoor man. Watch the way he walks over rough ground, and study his fire and his knife."

Most sportsmen would flunk that last test; their knives are either dull as hoes, or are Hollywood bowies that should never be seriously unsheathed.

I still carry a hunting knife sometimes, not that I expect to join battle with a crippled bear and cut my way out of jeopardy. But a thin, fixed blade is fine for slicing bacon, filleting fish, spearing baked potatoes, or cutting through the H-bone of a deer's pelvis. Such a knife shouldn't be long; a six-inch blade is plenty and a five-inch blade is even better.

But most of your outdoor needs may be served with a good pocketknife. It's admittedly tough to use in extreme cold and is easily lost, but it's compact and handy and I've even hog-dressed deer with such knives.

The so-called "combination" knives are miserable things; the blades are seldom of good design and most of the gadgets are worthless. I like a one-bladed knife with a white grip that is easy to see. Stag grips are too dark, and easily chipped and broken.

My first love is the "clip" blade, a graceful, narrow design that's easily honed and has a lot of working edge. At the bottom of my list are the "saber" and "pen" blades — old styles that deserve to grow no older. Whatever the shape of your blade, it should be thin and easily sharpened. A thick blade is stronger, but who's going to punch a safe with a jackknife? A knife is to cut with — not pry, chisel, throw or drive screws.

Until a couple of years ago I had always avoided stainless steel blades, believing that rustproof steel is unnatural, like a dog with a hot nose. Then I acquired a fine stainless steel pocketknife that has worked out splendidly. It holds an edge well, is immune to rust, has a thin sharp blade, and an ivory grip that can't be lost on a dusky riverbank.

That's one knife of many. There's one in my tacklebag, one in the chop box, and always one in my pocket. All have well-oiled springs and are extremely sharp, for I found long ago that a dull knife is dangerous.

My grandsire was a gambler and auctioneer who spent good weather on the porch with his constant companion, a dour Mesquakie 'breed named Barney. They never talked much. About all they ever did was look at their watches and hone their knives.

One of my earliest memories is of the Colonel's long shanks and the patient, silken whisper of steel on stone. I once asked: "Grampaw, why are you always sharpening your knife?"

"Because nothing dull has got any worth above ground, boy," came the reply.

I've learned since that there's a double-jointed joy in keeping a sharp blade, and my granddad shared only half his secret with me. Honing a knife gives you a chance to mull things over, to chew on your plans and dreams, and trick the womenfolk with an illusion of sober industry.

froze fer meat

IT STARTED at a high school picnic when we were teasing the girls with a big bullsnake. One of them screamed: "Why did you catch that horrid thing?" and Simp hollered back: "We're gonna *eat* it!"

Simp only said that for effect, but there was no turning back. We were committed. So we skinned the snake, cut it up, and spitted it on a stick to roast beside the marshmallows. Reveling in the girlish shrieks, we ate it.

It wasn't bad. Roast bullsnake, as I recall, gets bigger with the chewing and tastes something like a setting hen that's drowned in a horse trough. But it isn't bad eating when you're fifteen, hungry, and girls are watching you be brave.

For the next two years — more from wanting to be mountain men than from being hungry — we went on a binge of Injun cookery. If it walked, crawled, flew, swam or ran, we ate it. We chewed our way through a regiment of blackbirds, crows, robins, bugs, muskrats, skunks, groundhogs, bobcats, mussels, hawks and snakes. Some of this eating was a little rank, but much of it was pretty good and we learned a lot.

To this day, walking in from a hungry fishing trip, I may catch large grasshoppers, de-leg them, nip off the tips of the large thighs, and pull out the delicate slivers of meat. We never did learn to like fresh-water clams, but maybe we weren't handling them right. Crawdads are delicious, but mean a lot more cleaning than eating.

One of our big surprises was skunk. Older skunks tend to be a bit beetley in flavor, but a young animal tastes a lot like prime 'possum which, in turn, is sort of like pork. A man can do a lot worse than eating young skunk.

Same thing with muskrat, beaver and groundhog. I still think the finest wild meat I've ever eaten was a young muskrat done to a turn over a slow hickory fire in a trapper's camp. It's sweet, delicate, tender, and goes mighty well after you've laid about fifty drown sets in a November river.

Eating crow, blackbird, starling or hawk is just eating bird, and that's about all you can say for it. It's O.K. for a change, but it's nothing you'd get addicted to.

To capture the spirit of all this, we never put these critters into pies or stews. We took them straight, turned over a slow fire, for two reasons: (1) we owed at least that much to Jim Bridger, and (2) our mothers wouldn't allow the stuff into their kitchens, anyway. These experiments were so successful that we started calling each other "Ol' Hoss" and saying, "Waugh! This chile is froze fer meat!" We were budding mountain men, ready for anything, and so it was that one day we tried eating fox.

It was a big old dog fox, trapped in mid-February with romance on his mind and a winter's hard hunting behind him. He smelt like a sweaty civet cat, and under the thick fur we could feel the bands and packs of winter-hardened muscle. He promised to be about as toothsome as a belt knife, but we took him home anyway, butchered him and fried him on the laundry stove in the basement.

I'm here to testify that foxes taste just like they smell.

That was the rankest, meanest, sorriest meat that ever soured a frying pan. But it accomplished what scolding mothers and shuddering girl friends could never do — it converted us from mountain men into normal, small town boys. We knew when we were licked. That old fox was stronger and tougher than the best of us.

on crows

EVEN IF you don't care much for the crow, you have to give him his due. I've always had a deep, almost reverent awe for the raucous old rascal — the sort of feeling that I usually reserve for space scientists and extremely angry women.

For one thing, the crow has nearly every hand turned against him but gets along just fine. Men bomb him, poison him and gun him down, but he still flourishes and apparently there's not much we can do about it.

There's a reason for this — the crow is just about the endpoint of avian evolution. He's gone about as far as a bird can go, and is splendidly equipped for survival under an immense range of diet and living conditions. Hardfeathered and sleek, he has a voice like a woodrasp and a mind like a diamond.

He even makes a good pet. But be ready for anything, for comparing a crow to a canary is like matching Mort Sahl with Mortimer Snerd. I knew a pet crow that learned to bark like a dog, and drove the neighborhood pups out of their minds as he "wowfed" at passers-by from the porch roof, keeping the local cats and door-to-door salesmen all stirred up.

Crows may be pretty good talkers. Jack Musgrove knew one back home that lived in a drugstore. The bird and the druggist played catch with little balls of tinfoil when business was slow. Whenever this druggist got mad, he would roar: "Jim, I'm gonna cut a big club and beat the daylights out of you!"

Jim would r'ar back on his perch, feign shocked dismay, and rasp: "Oh, don't do it! Don't *do* it! !"

A crow is at his cagey best in the wild. He knows hunters better than their wives do, and can easily calculate the midrange trajectory of a varmint rifle. Some naturalists believe that crows have a simple language and can even count up to five.

Because crows can usually out-think them in the field, hunters may festoon their roosts with bombs and blow everything to flinders after nightfall. But for crow carnage in the daytime, I'll nominate a couple of hired hands in northern Iowa who scorned such roost bombs. These two old Swedes, after using black powder one winter to split logs, decided to build a crow cannon.

They first scrounged several barrels of very bad eggs from the local hatchery. Then they wrapped a section of five-inch well casing with old baling wire and poured in a few cans of black powder and a couple of bushels of scrap piston rings that they had broken up with a borrowed axe. This done, they dug a deep foxhole behind the crow cannon and strung the eggs in long swaths through the cornfield that lay, like a slumbering Armageddon, within the cone of fire.

The next morning there were a few crows feeding on the fragrant eggs; on the second morning there were even more, and on the third day the field was black with birds.

On the fourth day — it's still called "Bloody Thursday" in that part of the country — our two heroes touched off the fuse and took cover.

Triple mischief — three fledgling crows aligned on a tree branch. Noisy, hungry and alert, these are the child prodigies of the bird world.

Old-timers say that the sun was obscured all morning and that odd parts of the crow cannon rained down on two townships, and that an acre of field didn't need plowing that spring. The dead crows allegedly filled a wagon, and the two hired men modestly accepted a huge bounty payment and an enduring niche in Sac County legend.

romany rides again

IT HAS BEEN SAID that an outdoor life creates either monsters or poets.

I wouldn't know about that, for I've met neither in my ramblings around the boondocks. But I'm sure that the outdoors somehow shapes odd characters, and that fresh air enhances them. And since I'm outside quite a bit, I'm always stumbling across characters that are drawn much larger than life. Like the Roamers of Romany at Little Wall Lake.

It was a cool gray day in early April, and although the frost was weeks out of the earth, its bite still lingered in the wind. The sky had been clear when I left home that morning, but by the time I reached Little Wall the rain was starting again. I drove down the gravelled road at the south end of the lake, parked just off the shoulder about a hundred yards from the main highway, and headed upshore.

I was making a phenological study of the lake, determining the order and dates of appearance of aquatic plants. Little Wall is only about a mile around, but it took me nearly five hours to work the shoreline and check on emerging arrowhead, flag, threesquare bulrush and cattail. Except for a few winter-thin muskrats and some ragged squadrons of sprigs and bluebills that were having a wild party in midmarsh, I was alone.

By late afternoon I'd had it. I completed the circuit of the lake and returned to the car, tossed packbasket and wet coat into the trunk, slid under the wheel, and looked to Story City and a bait of hot coffee and buttered *kringlas*.

But as soon as I let out the clutch, I knew I had trouble. The rear wheels spun hub-deep into the soft ground and my car was peacefully interred in the lakeshore.

I was standing beside the mired car, swearing quietly and trying to dope out a course of action, when company arrived.

There were three ancient sedans, laboring through the rain beneath loads of furniture, stoves, duffle and tarpaulins. The leading car stopped nearby with a clatter of burned valves and the driver got out and walked over. He was a thin, swart man with a mop of black ringlets and a face as benevolent as a stropped razor. He was wearing a lavender silk shirt, a pair of old army pants, and pointed yellow shoes. People began to swarm out of the cars behind him — young dark men, old dark men, dark women and girls with bright kerchiefs, and a crew of dark, ragged kids that included one improbable youngster with golden hair.

"Watsa matter, sport?" said the dark driver with the yellow shoes. "You steeck the car?"

I didn't think that deserved an answer, and the gypsy chief stood there in the drizzle in his lavender silk shirt and surveyed the situation.

"I sink I can help you, sport," he said finally. "You got moony?"

I was loaded. Two eighty-five in cash and another two dollars in a government travel check. I told him I had money.

"Den I know I help you. 'Ow moch you pay to gait pooled from ze mod?"

I did some fast figuring and said I'd go two bucks' worth.

By this time he had been joined by three other men who looked things over and discussed me rapidly in Hungarian or something.

"Eet's a dill, sport," said the chief, and scuttled back to his old sedan. He opened the trunk, threw some blankets and bags and stuff out on the wet gravel, and emerged with some rope.

They jockeyed the old sedan into towing position and found that the rope wasn't long enough. More digging through duffle, and more Hungarian discussion. As I stood there in the mud and dolefully watched all this, an unoccupied gypsy sidled up to me and said:

" 'Ey, *gorgio*. 'Ow you get zat fender busted in like zat?"

I told him that a corncrib had hit it.

"I feex zat fender good, eh *gorgio*?"

"Leave it like it is."

"Nah-h-h. Zat's no dom good. I feex heem."

"Look. I don't have much money and you don't have any tools. Forget it."

"Ah got zee tools. 'Ow moch moony you got?"

"Couple bucks. Forget it."

But he was already on his way back to the cars, and in a few seconds he came slopping back through the deepening mud carrying a heavy rubber hammer and a leather sandbag — the tools of a professional body man. My respect for Romany deepened.

"Two bocks and Ah feex eet swell, sport."

It had to be done sometime, anyway. And it would still leave me enough for coffee and *kringlas*.

By this time there were gypsies all over the place. Two were digging beneath the front axle of my car with army entrenching spades and attaching a length of chain, another was digging mud away from the rear wheels, and the repair contingent was at work on the mashed hind fender. A couple of others were cutting state-owned willows down by the lake to make a corduroy on the soft gravel road for the venerable tow-car. Most of the kids, including the improbable blonde, were up by the highway scrounging for old bottles with refund value. The women were yelling around, kids were screaming in the distance, and the men were shouting things that were cusswords in anybody's language. It was the busiest day on Little Wall Lake since the opening of duck season.

By the time the digging gypsies had finished, the tow-rope gypsies had everything spliced together, the willow-cutting gypsies had a track built, and the ancient sedan was unloaded and ready to pull. At that precise instant, the body repair gypsies popped the last dent out of the fender and headed back to the road with their tools.

There was a piercing whistle, the kids came whooping in from the highway with a few coke bottles, relayed them to the women without breaking stride, and crowded in behind my car to help push. I got in, shifted into low gear, and the unified forces of Norway and Romany coaxed my howling car up to the gravel.

No one stood around to savor victory. Kids, shovels, body tools and bottles were stashed away in the recesses of the old cars while a few of the men freed the tow-rope. Oblivious of the mud and rain on his lavender silk shirt, the chief approached me and said:

"Dat'll be four bocks, sport."

I told him that I had $2.85 in cash, and that the two-dollar government check could be cashed anywhere. He studied the check carefully and called over his colleagues for another conference in Hungarian-or-something. They finally decided to trust the government and gathered around to watch me endorse the check.

"Wan leetle theeng," said the chief. "We don' usual geet paid weeth ze chack."

A murmer of dark laughter there in the rain, white teeth flashing.

"So dere'll be a leetle theeng of two-bits for casheeng ze chack."

I gave them the check and fished two dollars and a quarter out of my pocket. This cleared the board, and I pocketed the rest. You can buy a lot of coffee and *kringlas* in Story City for sixty cents.

All in all, I felt pretty good about the whole thing. I'd always heard that gypsies have a genius for attaching anything that isn't tied down or locked up. I had this on no less authority than my grandfather, a gifted horsetrader and poker player who — despite his sharp dealings — religiously eschewed business with gypsies. But I had always discounted gypsy stories as a lot of granny talk. And here was a case in point; I had just dealt with gypsies, hadn't been robbed, and had money left over.

So I was standing in the rain, jingling my sixty cents and feeling pretty good about the wariness of us *gorgios,* when one of the women walked up. She was all rigged out for the mitt camp of a carnival, complete with scarlet bandana and — so help me — golden earrings. All she needed was a tambourine filled with tea leaves.

"Look into your future, meester?" she said.

"How much?" I asked, although I really knew.

"Seexty cents," she said.

It didn't take me long to get home, because there was no stop in Story City for hot coffee and buttered *kringlas.* On the way, driving through the cold drizzle of the April dusk, I pondered the wisdom of grandfathers.

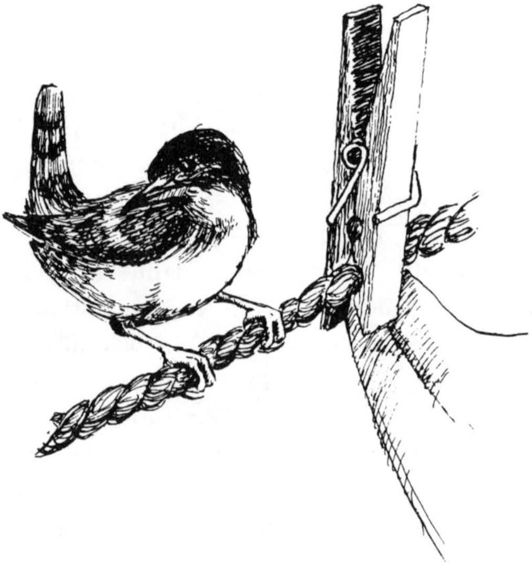

the small brown bird

WHEN I'M TOO RICKETY to hunt, and find more pleasure in polishing my guns than shooting them, I have many things to do.

I'd like to make fine gunstocks — gleaming custom work that will make a gun nut catch his breath. Maybe I'll make duck and goose decoys, too, and give them away to youngsters who are just starting out. I'll do a lot of reading and fishing and puttering.

But more than anything else, I'll keep an eye on the birds.

I've gotten behind on this, because lately it seems there's always a bass to be caught or a goose pit to dig. But it's a thing that needs doing, for I can't fool my grandchildren with long, thundering Outdoor Stories if I don't even know the small brown bird in the lilacs.

That bird has bothered me lately, because it proves that I'm not an outdoorsman. A hunter and fisherman, yes, and even a pretty good mushroom man, but not a real outdoorsman. If I were, I'd know about obscure things like mosses, ferns, wildflowers and small brown birds.

Most hunters and fishermen are like that; they know the big things like bears and geese and steelheads, but may feel that the small ones are beneath their dignity. Too many think that songbirds are strictly for aging maiden ladies and men with lace on their binoculars.

Birdwatching is a gentle sport. Maybe that's why some anglers and hunters scorn it, for most of us like to imagine ourselves as all-wool men with no time for such things. But if a Sioux dog soldier could find dignity in knowing birds and their legends, why can't a weekend quailhunter?

When you get to the nub of it, hunters and birdwatchers are much alike. Essentially, they both love the same thing and both may be unrealistic about it. The hunter may be blind to everything but bag limits and never see the wonders he walks among. The birdwatcher may be living in a Bambi world that doesn't recognize winter kills, predation, or violent death.

But now and then you'll meet men who are both birdwatchers and hunters. These are real outdoorsmen. I've known only a few — guys who could name rocks, find food roots, talk to thrushes, and still wipe my eye in a duck blind. They are usually happy men, for their interests are broad enough to span boyhood and old age.

I shall try to be like this for I admire wildlife in any form, and birds are pristine wildlife just as surely as the lobo or the grizzly. They are all around us, and even while we mourn the passing of the wilderness we have the wilderness birds at our elbows.

They are one part of the old wild scene that is still found everywhere. The grizzlies have gone. But the wrens that scolded them may still scold you from the clothesline, and the robin in Central Park is the same bird that sang to Dan'l Boone.

outdoor wishbooks

SOME MEN escape reality by chewing snoose, watching girls, or practicing their fast draw. Me, I'll take sporting goods catalogues every time.

They're wonderful, these outdoor wishbooks that extol rods, lures, guns and boots. They're special license to open the season months ahead of time. In winter you read about fishing stuff; in summer you study hunting gear. In between are idle months of compasses, crow calls, folding grills and canvas toilets.

Some of my favorite wishbooks are the ones showing costly things. Now, I have as much use for a salmon rod or a Mount Everest tent as a pig has for pockets, but it's a pleasure being exposed to them. There's a vicarious thrill in buying four-bit bootlaces that lie overpage from a hundred-dollar trout rod.

But my first loves are those salty, two-fisted wishbooks that cater to the little man. Free catalogues with low prices, plenty of big pictures, and some of the most vigorous prose that ever rolled roughshod over a competitor:

> Users of our Surescratch Watertight Matchbox include Old Woodsmen and Others. These Matchboxes have saved countless lives in the Cruel North and our president, Mr. J. L. Custard, would not set foot from his office without one. Knurled for a sure grip with frozen hands, the seamless Surescratch is made special for us by the nation's foremost maker of Watertight Matchboxes. By comparison, our competitors offer only Trash Matchboxes. $0.98, plus freight.

What real sportsman could resist that?

I'll go as high as a quarter for a new wishbook and I'm at the top of at least twenty sucker lists. The month doesn't go by without finding a new catalogue in my mail.

My first move is to grab it and sneak off like a bird dog that's just eaten a quail, taking the wishbook to my workshop where I can look it over with glacier-slow thoroughness. After years of this I can reel off the cost of anything from shikari hats to folding bathtubs.

Once in awhile I even order something. Although I've been buying from wishbooks for a long time, it's always the same. There's a brief, painful travail with Dycie and then the equally painful wait for the postman. For whenever you order from an outdoor wishbook, it's Christmas all over again and you're ten years old and waiting for that first BB gun.

Women can't grasp this. Taking time to fish and hunt is strange enough, but taking time getting ready to spend money getting ready to take time to fish and hunt is utterly beyond them. Nothing in a woman's background equips her for such a thing.

There are dangers in such buying, and a man might be better off buying merchandise he can examine. But no store could be so adventurous, and no clerk alive can spout the sterling, livesaving virtues of the Surescratch Watertight Matchbox so well as J. L. Custard's Annual Fall Outdoor Catalogue.

a place to loaf

IF MY INCOME ever exceeds my outgo, I'm going to have a special room.

It'll be in a house just below the crest of a hill that breaks the northwest wind — a room above a bright, brawling river that I can hear in the evening when I hoist my feet up on the desk, scratch where I itch, and smoke my pipe.

The room will be on the east side of the house so that it catches the morning sun but not the afternoon glare, and there'll be a sort of French door that opens out on a trail shaded by rock maples.

It'll be a big, airy room with windows all along the outer wall; not picture windows, but ones that can be swung open to let in the breeze and the noise of the river.

That room will be a cache of my favorite junk arranged just as I want it. One wall will be a book case, a floor-to-ceiling library with papers and books on conservation, mammals, birds, snakes, fish and dogs. The bottom shelf will be fun books by Twain, Cobb, Kipling, Bill Adams and Tomlinson, and cartoon books by Punch, J. R. Williams and Charley Russell.

I'd like to make the floor of either puncheon or flagstone, and partly cover it with a big braided rug. At the window will be the desk that isn't a desk at all, but a massive trestle table of walnut made of a lightning-felled tree from Allamakee County.

On the table will be the driftwood lamp I made from an Arkansas sassafras root that smelled like rock candy when the saw was put to it. And beneath will be an old Pima rug for Kelly — the huge, worthless Irish setter that has raised three children and likes to sleep where they can't step on him.

Across the room will be a stone fireplace. I'm not being rustic, but a neat brick fireplace wouldn't be fair to that room. I know just the stone, too — part of a ledge tempered and stained by a trout stream that has gone dry.

There will be many pictures. Frank Miller's cartoons of his wonderful weather prophet, Chief Fabulous Feather, and Dycie's moonlit painting of massed snow and blue geese rising from the Plum Creek Washout on the Missouri.

There'll be snapshots of friends holding fish with wisecracks written beneath them, and pen and ink sketches of clammers' johnboats on the river. But the place of honor will be held by that picture of the lecherous old raccoon leering at his lady love in a tree, with the Dutchman's caption "Old John Madson Coon" that makes me laugh and think of walleyed pike whenever I look at it. Beside this will hang the stuffed canvasback drake, his head dangling from a string and labelled: "Blowed his haid plumb off, *but hain't he a dandy!!*"

In the corner will be a pine cabinet for my rods and my shotguns and rifles, plain work guns whose stocks glow with tung oil and endless rubbing.

There'll be a deep leather chair for you, and an old scarred bench where we can slop coffee and no one will care.

There'll be a big coffeepot in the fireplace, the kind granddad kept on the back of the wood range when he told roaring sea stories about the old whaling days out of Bergen. For once we'll have all the black coffee we can drink, and maybe a bait of smoked sturgeon or *lutefisk* to go with it.

And I know what will happen. The womenfolk will find my room just as they always do and although they'll poke fun at it, that's where they'll gather to sit and listen to the river.

But don't let that stop you; come on out. We'll shoo the ladies away and sit by the fire and talk of many things, honing our knives and watching Old Kelly twitch as he breaks forty-bird coveys in his sleep.